KU-637-415

**Ray's arm at her waist didn't let her go far. Long fingers traced the keyhole in her bodice. "Did I tell you how lovely you look tonight?"**

"You did." And the desire in his eyes had repeated the message over and over throughout the night.

Lauren had wanted to make him notice her—and she had succeeded, all right. To the point where it had almost backfired on her. The searing weight of his gaze had followed her all night, and her body had responded with heightened awareness until she could barely concentrate. There she had stood, rubbing elbows with the rich and powerful, and she'd struggled to put together coherent sentences. Fortunately the fact that a friend of the mayor's wife had heard of By Arrangement had caught her attention and grounded her in the conversation so she didn't actually embarrass herself.

The desire was back in his eyes now, burning brighter than ever, making her nerves tingle and her body heat. She much preferred seeing passion over pain in his sea-blue eyes. And, oh, he smelled good.

She missed being held by him. So, with luxury surrounding her, New York lit up at her feet, and a hard man pulling her close, she surrendered her control.

Rising on her toes, she kissed the hard line of his jaw. "Are you just going to look? Or do you plan to do something about it?"

**Dear Reader**

Are you loving the new glitz and glamour aspect of Mills & Boon® Romance as much as I am? I've been to Europe and Hollywood, and in *A Pregnancy, a Party & a Proposal* I'm jetting off to New York. This trip is part personal experience, part research.

I *have* been to the Big Apple and stayed in a hotel on Times Square. There's no place like it on earth. And it's exactly as manic as it seems on TV and in the movies.

The research came in for the Statue of Liberty. I've been to the island, but never up to the crown. The first time I saw the iconic statue it was covered in scaffolding while being restored. The second time was after 9/11 and the tour to the crown was closed. Armed security guards even chased people off the grassy area surrounding the statue. I didn't get to the crown, but I must say it was a memorable visit.

In *A Pregnancy, a Party & a Proposal* the trip to New York is an exciting first for my heroine, Lauren Randall, but a painful return home for my hero, Ray Donovan. If this is your first 'trip' to New York I hope I do it justice.

Enjoy the glitz!

*Teresa Carpenter*

# A PREGNANCY,
# A PARTY
# & A PROPOSAL

BY
TERESA CARPENTER

All rights reserved including the right of reproduction in whole
or in part in any form. This edition is published by arrangement with
Harlequin Books S.A.

This is a work of fiction. Names, characters, places, locations and
incidents are purely fictional and bear no relationship to any real
life individuals, living or dead, or to any actual places, business
establishments, locations, events or incidents. Any resemblance is
entirely coincidental.

This book is sold subject to the condition that it shall not, by way of
trade or otherwise, be lent, resold, hired out or otherwise circulated
without the prior consent of the publisher in any form of binding or
cover other than that in which it is published and without a similar
condition including this condition being imposed on the subsequent
purchaser.

® and TM are trademarks owned and used by the trademark owner
and/or its licensee. Trademarks marked with ® are registered with the
United Kingdom Patent Office and/or the Office for Harmonisation in
the Internal Market and in other countries.

First published in Great Britain 2015
by Mills & Boon, an imprint of Harlequin (UK) Limited,
Eton House, 18-24 Paradise Road, Richmond, Surrey, TW9 1SR

© 2015 Teresa Carpenter

ISBN: 978-0-263-25742-7

Harlequin (UK) Limited's policy is to use papers that are natural,
renewable and recyclable products and made from wood grown in
sustainable forests. The logging and manufacturing processes conform
to the legal environmental regulations of the country of origin.

Printed and bound in Great Britain
by CPI Antony Rowe, Chippenham, Wiltshire

**Teresa Carpenter** believes that with love and family anything is possible. She writes in a Southern California coastal city surrounded by her large family. Teresa loves writing about babies and grandmas. Her books have rated Top Picks by *RT Book Reviews*, and have been nominated Best Romance of the Year on some review sites. If she's not at a family event, she's reading, or writing her next grand romance.

### Books by Teresa Carpenter

*Her Boss by Arrangement*
*Stolen Kiss from a Prince*
*The Making of a Princess*
*Baby Under the Christmas Tree*
*The Sheriff's Doorstep Baby*
*The Playboy's Gift*
*Sheriff Needs a Nanny*
*The Boss's Surprise Son*

**Visit the author profile page at
www.millsandboon.co.uk for more titles**

| MORAY COUNCIL LIBRARIES & INFO.SERVICES | |
|---|---|
| 20 38 82 88 | |
| **Askews & Holts** | |
| RF RF | |
| | |

For Gabrielle, the younger twin,
pragmatic, dedicated, witty, and a very hard worker.
You're going to make a great pharmacist.
I love you, babe.

# CHAPTER ONE

"'TWO LINES MEANS PREGNANT.'" Lauren Randall read the early detection instructions. "'One line, not pregnant.'"

Simple enough. Perched on the side of the bed in a long blue robe, heart beating a mile a millisecond, she scrunched her eyes closed—a cowardly act entirely unlike her—and then opened them to look at the stick.

Two lines.

She blinked. Looked again. Still two lines.

"Oh, boy." She blew out a pent-up breath. Her mind spun with the news. She was going to be a mother. Strolling to the bedroom's picture window, she stared unseeing at the Pacific Ocean.

Her hand went to her waist. She was expecting a baby.

Ray Donovan's baby. Mind-boggling. This type of thing didn't happen to her. She was too organized, too controlled. She didn't have unprotected sex. She *hadn't* had unprotected sex. But a broken condom might have changed her life…forever.

She glanced at the stick in her hand. Yep, still two lines.

"Oh, my." A baby.

A tiny part of her was thrilled at the knowledge. She was having a *baby*! Would he or she have Lauren's blond hair and light brown eyes? Or Ray's sandy, slightly darker locks and blue eyes?

Just thinking about it sent the more rational side of her reeling. A child was not in her current five-year plan.

Certainly not a child with a domineering man incapable of standing still for two whole minutes.

The sound of pounding drew her gaze down. Below her the lush garden of the Santa Barbara estate was being transformed into a wedding paradise. The day had dawned sunny and bright and, according to the meteorologists, might reach seventy degrees. Given it was Valentine's Day, they were lucky. February weather could be unpredictable in Southern California.

The event promised to be spectacular. On the edge of the property a white-columned gazebo stood against a backdrop of green hedges and long-standing trees, beyond which the vast Pacific Ocean flowed on forever, symbolic of the unending devotion about to be declared.

Short columns on which sat rose ball topiaries created the aisle. White chairs with silver sashes provided seating for the guests. A huge white tent graced the middle of the lawn and wood flooring had been put down. The tent-poles had been encased in columns to match the gazebo and thousands of white lights were being draped across the ceiling to give the impression of dancing under the stars.

More rose topiaries acted as centerpieces on the round tables at the dining end. Curved couches ringed the dance floor at the other end. The overall vision was elegant, yet understated, and *her* By Arrangement team had pulled it off beautifully.

Co-owners of By Arrangement, Lauren and Tori had both taken on new assistants at the start of the year. They were working the event, but the rest of the jobs had vendors in place, thus freeing their staff to attend as guests.

Shortly Lauren would be walking down the aisle toward Ray. Not as bride to his groom, but as maid of honor to his best man. Today was not her big day, but her twin's. Tori would marry the man she loved in a romantic ocean-view ceremony in a little over two hours.

If that gave Lauren a pinch of envy it was only because her sister was so happy. Difficult not to want that for herself.

But it was only a pinch. After a bad scare in college, she'd put her career in front of romance. So far she had few regrets. Lauren liked where she was in life. Of course she'd need to recalibrate now she was going to have a child to consider.

So, a wedding for her sister and a baby for her. The timing of the discovery was extraordinary. Was this some kind of karmic message? Or perhaps a spiritual nudge?

Now, *there* was a cosmic joke—because "marriage" and "Ray" were two words that didn't belong in the same sentence, or even paragraph. Heck, they wouldn't be in the same novel.

And if she hadn't been playing ostrich—again, totally unlike her—she would have known she was pregnant a week ago. She'd certainly suspected, with the nausea and the tenderness in her breasts. But she'd been busy and in denial—a slick combination for avoiding the inevitable.

There'd been too much to do, what with last-minute details for the wedding and family coming into town for the rehearsal. Seeing Ray again was what had prompted her to pick up the early pregnancy testing kit. She couldn't contemplate walking down the aisle to him without knowing the truth. Not that knowing the truth helped now that it was a yes.

Well, no time to brood about it now.

Tossing the stick in the trash, she moved to the closet to take down her dress. It was past time to join Tori and their mother in Tori's room to get ready.

A knock sounded at the door. Carrying the dress, she opened the door to her mother.

Like Lauren, her mom already had her hair and make-up done. Garrett, Tori's fiancé and owner of Obsidian Studios, had arranged for three professional hairstylists and make-up artists to come to the house to prepare the wedding party for the event. Her mom looked lovely, with her hair swept up in a sleek French twist and the expert application of cosmetics. But then she looked just as pretty with no make-up and her hair in a ponytail.

To Lauren, she was just Mom.

"Oh, Mom." She launched herself into Liz Randall's arms, letting the scent of lavender comfort her.

The news of her baby nearly tripped off Lauren's tongue. She pressed her lips together to prevent the words from spilling. This was Tori's special day. Lauren would never do anything to disrupt her twin's wedding day.

"Hey." Her mother's arms closed around her, careful not to crush the dress she held. "Are you okay?"

"Yes," she lied. She wouldn't be okay until this day was over and the certainty of running into Ray no longer existed. And, truthfully, the hug did make her feel better. She forced her mind to switch gears. "Our girl is getting married."

"I know." Liz gave her another squeeze before stepping back. "She won't be right next door anymore, but we have to remember we're not losing her—we're gaining a new son and brother." She tweaked the ends of Lauren's hair and studied her closely. "Are you sure you're okay? You're a little pale."

"I'm fine." Lauren hooked her arm through her mother's as they walked down the hall to the master suite. "I'll still miss her."

"She's your partner. You'll see her nearly every day."

"It won't be the same."

No, and their lives were going to change even more drastically than her mom knew.

"Different, yes, but in a good way." Liz was a glass half-full gal. "Especially when we start getting little ones to play with. You two will be twenty-nine in a couple of months. I've waited a long time to be a grandmother."

Yeah, well, her wait was nearly up.

"Oh!" Liz exclaimed. "Maybe she'll have twins."

Lauren's stomach did a little flip. She swallowed hard. Okay, she wasn't ready to think about having twins.

Down the way a door opened and Ray Donovan stepped into the hall. He wore jeans and a muscle-clinging green T-shirt. His shaggy dark blond hair had been trimmed considerably since she'd seen him last night. It was brushed back at the sides and a little wild on top. He looked entirely too yummy for her peace of mind.

He hesitated at the head of the stairs, his blue gaze traveling between her and her mother. He lifted his camera, aimed it in their direction.

"Ray, stop that. We're not dressed yet. Where are you going?" Her mother pointed to the car keys in his hand. "You should be getting ready."

He pocketed the keys. "I have an errand. I'll be back in plenty of time." With a last glance at Lauren, which she avoided, he headed downstairs.

For a wild moment she wondered how he would deal with twins. But her mind refused to wrap around the concept so she pulled her focus back to Tori.

"Mom, I think we should let her get through the wedding before we have her barefoot and pregnant."

"Sweetheart…" Liz patted Lauren's hand "…who are you kidding? Tori will be barefoot before the end of the night."

The statement was so true they were giggling when the door in front of them opened and Tori stood there in sexy curls, a silky white robe, and bare feet. "Where have you two been?"

Lauren met her mother's golden gaze, so like her own, and they both burst out laughing.

Ray Donovan shifted his wide shoulders in the custom-made tuxedo. Weddings gave him hives. *Been there, almost did that, never plan to do it again.* A fact not even his good buddy Garrett knew. It had happened so long ago Ray liked to pretend it had never happened at all.

Pacing the study, or "the groom's room", as Lauren's new assistant had corrected him, Ray twitched at his tie. He was slowly suffocating.

Thinking of Lauren didn't help at all. Contrary woman. The honey-eyed blond was the hottest armful he'd ever held, but way too stubborn for his taste when they weren't locked in a clinch. Their fling, for want of a better word, was over.

Until two days ago he hadn't seen her since Christmas, when she'd called time on their trysts.

How stunning to realize he'd actually missed her. But any hope of expending his nervous energy by reigniting the chemistry between them while they were hooked up for the wedding festivities had fizzled out when she had refused to meet his gaze at the rehearsal. Or any time since.

*Okay. Message received.*

All for the best. In spite of his hopeful initial reaction, he'd been truly unnerved as he'd watched her walk down the aisle toward him. The sight had been a punch to the gut. He hadn't stopped twitching since. Confirmation that he'd been smart to keep it casual, to let her end things between them.

He paused in front of a gilded mirror. He smoothed his short sandy hair back into place and straightened his tie. *Pull it together,* he silently chided himself. *You're sounding more like a wuss than a director known for going into the trenches with his stuntmen and actors.*

"Relax," Garrett said from his place behind the desk. "Anyone would think it was you getting married instead of me."

"I don't know how you can be so calm."

Ray dropped into the chair in front of the desk, picked up his camera and shot the groom. To occupy his hands, as well as his mind, he'd decided to give the bride and groom the gift of an insider's perspective on their wedding: pictures and videos no photographer would have access to.

"The waiting is excruciating. How much longer before this gig gets going?"

Garrett's gaze shifted to the mantel clock. "Soon. And it's easy to be calm when you're sure of what you're doing."

"Marriage is a trap for the unwary. Standing up there in front of everyone is a lonely place to be."

Okay, he knew that was warped even as the words slipped out. His memories had no place here.

"I won't be alone." Garrett laughed off the outrageous comment. "I'll be joined by the woman I love. Until then you'll be by my side."

Garrett opened the bottom drawer in the solid oak desk and pulled out a bottle of aged whiskey and a single crystal glass. After pouring a good dollop into the glass, he pushed it across the oak surface to Ray.

"Maybe this will help settle your nerves."

"No, thanks." Ray turned down the shot. Normally he'd accept and relish the burn. Today he'd remain stone-cold sober. The way he felt, adding alcohol was not a good idea.

"I don't understand you, dude." Garrett shook his head. "You're the one who told me I'd be safe with Tori."

"It's easy to see she makes you happy." Ray ran a hand over his jaw. Just because marriage wasn't for him didn't mean others couldn't benefit from the bond. "And of course you have that whole Spidey sense of approval going for you."

Apparently the twins were natural matchmakers and got a special "feeling" when they saw two people who belonged together. Lauren had gotten the feeling about Garrett and Tori, but hadn't said anything until after they were engaged.

Garrett arched a dark eyebrow. "Mock if you want. I'm reaping the rewards."

"Sorry. The truth is you deserve the best. Don't mind me—weddings make me twitchy."

"So you said when I asked you to be my best man. Thanks for doing this for me."

"You're the closest thing I have to a brother. Of course I'm here for you."

"What's your deal anyway?"

Ray shook his head. "Ancient history. Too depressing for the occasion."

Too depressing, period. He didn't talk or think about those times.

A knock sounded at the door and Lauren's assistant stuck her head in. "It's time, gentlemen."

"We'll be right there," Garrett assured her, and surged to his feet. He looked at Ray as he rose too. "Are you ready for this?"

Ray waved Garrett forward, then clapped him on the back when he passed. "Let's get you hitched."

Outside, Ray stood at his friend's side in the shade of the gazebo as music filled the air and the bridal party started toward them. Nick Randall escorted his mother to the front row. As soon as they were seated, Lauren began her journey down the rose-strewn runner.

Ray couldn't take his eyes off her. She wore a strapless, figure-hugging silver gown, showing her curves to sweet advantage. The fading sun gleamed in golden curls swept to one side, leaving one creamy shoulder bare. She grew more stunning the closer she got.

He completely missed the bride walking down the aisle as his gaze lingered on the maid of honor. Watching her, he remembered their first heated encounter in the laundry room of his home on Thanksgiving. Desire stirred.

Not wanting to embarrass himself, or his friend, he turned his attention—and his camera—to the ceremony. The officiate spoke, and then Garrett and Tori exchanged the poignant vows they'd written themselves. Weddings might make Ray itch, but as a film director he recognized powerful dialogue when he heard it.

He received the signal to hand over the rings. Garrett kissed his bride. The officiate introduced the couple as Mr. and Mrs. Black. And finally the time came for Ray to touch Lauren as they moved to follow the couple up the aisle in a reverse procession.

As before, she refused to look at him as he linked her arm around his.

"You look beautiful." He laid his hand over hers and squeezed. Forget her decree. He wasn't ready to let her go yet. Changing her mind was exactly the distraction he needed.

She bunched her fingers into a fist, but didn't look at him.

"You girls outdid yourselves with the decorations."

She rolled her amber eyes. "You could care less about the decorations."

"Not true. As a director, I admire a well-organized scene."

"I'm sure Tori will be glad you approve. It's her vision."

They reached the end of the aisle. Lauren immediately pulled free of him.

"Don't wander off. We'll be doing photos in a moment."

"Yes," he tossed out with droll humor. "I got a copy of the itinerary."

That drew her gaze as she narrowed her eyes at him. "Behave."

He lifted an eyebrow. "Where's the fun in that?" He leaned close, inhaled her sweet scent—honeysuckle and soap—and whispered, "Meet me in the laundry room in twenty minutes."

A blush added color to her rose-dusted cheeks. But, oh, such warm eyes weren't meant to give off chills. Her hands went to her shapely hips, but before she could speak she was drawn into a hug as friends and family descended on the wedding party.

"You're a piece of work," she managed in an aside between greetings. "What about your date?"

"I'm stag tonight." He shook hands and nodded as people stopped in front of him. In a short break between one guest and the next he sent her a sultry look over his shoulder. "There's been no one since you."

"What? I'm supposed to feel sorry for you?" She snorted, then had to paste on a smile when her grandmother gave her an odd look. "Spare me, please. You're a world-class director. You could have a woman on your arm with the snap of your fingers."

"I pine for you," he said, and lifted Grandma Randall's hand to his mouth to kiss her fingers. "So nice to meet you. It's easy to see where Tori gets her beauty."

The older woman twittered prettily and moved on.

"Flirt," Lauren admonished him.

He grinned. "She loved it."

"Only proves my point. You won't be alone for long."

"Come on—I barely know anyone." There were a few film industry people here, but the biggest portion of guests was made up of Tori's family and friends. "You're maid of honor to my best man. We're scripted to be together."

"Hmm. You've spent half the time behind that camera. I don't know why you need company at all."

Implying he was lacking at his duties? Why did he allow her to get to him? Yes, she was lovely, but he'd dated some of the most gorgeous women in the world. She was a bit of a brat, and she constantly challenged his authority. But one whiff of her scent and he could think of only one thing: getting her alone.

The thinning crowd shifted, bumping Lauren into Ray. He grabbed her to keep her from toppling. His fingers framed her hips as he drew her close.

He lowered his head and kissed the vulnerable curve

of her neck. "The laundry room door has a lock. We won't be gone long."

She melted against him. The corner of his mouth kicked up in satisfaction as he mentally tracked the fastest route to the utility room. They both had bedrooms inside, but the laundry room held sentimental value. Best of all, no one was likely to look for them there.

In the next instant she'd elbowed him in the gut and twisted from his grasp. "Hands off."

He immediately held his hands up in a sign of surrender. He looked at her more closely. "Are you okay? You're a little pale."

She looked away. "I'm fine. I just choose not to let my hormones rule me today. It's my sister's wedding. I'm not going to steal away with you."

Lauren's assistant appeared, ushering the wedding party back to the gazebo.

"No one will miss us after the photos are done."

"Just *stop*." She planted a hand in the middle of his chest and lifted a pleading gaze to him.

He stepped back. "Pardon me."

He'd never forced himself on a woman and he wouldn't start now. If she didn't care to act on the desire her stand-offishness couldn't completely disguise, he respected her decision. He'd only pursued her because she helped distract him from the wedding heebie-jeebies.

Shoulders back, he gestured her forward.

For the next twenty minutes he stood where instructed, smiled when told, and snapped his own shots when he wasn't needed. Finally the photographer released the wedding party. He trekked to the reception with Lauren's brother Nick.

They exchanged pleasantries. "How's work?" Ray asked.

"Busy. I know I shouldn't be happy about that." Nick ran the trauma unit at a Palm Springs hospital. "But I prefer action to twiddling my thumbs. How about you? Is there a new film I should be looking forward to?"

"I wrapped up *Gates of Peril* in December. It'll be out over the summer. I'm still in the planning stages of the next one."

"I'm going to hold you to that invite to a premier you issued at Thanksgiving. Not only will I enjoy the movie, it'll be serious chick points."

Nick introduced Ray to more family and he got some nice group footage. Lauren had a large, fun family. Grandma Randall did like to flirt. She snagged his arm and showed him off. It made him think of his own family. He owed his grandmother a call. She had raised him from the age of ten, when his parents had died in an auto accident. Her birthday was this week.

Having delayed as long as possible, he wandered over to the head table. Along the way a curvy redhead caught his eye. She showed her interest with a come-hither gaze. He kept on walking. He already had all the woman he could handle tonight.

At the head table he slid into his seat next to Lauren. Tori's parents sat on the other side of the happy couple. Unwilling to sit in uncomfortable silence for the duration of dinner, he turned on the charm.

He kept the conversation light and impersonal, which put Lauren at ease. Stories from the set were always entertaining, and he finally drew a laugh from his companion. It gave him almost as much satisfaction as when she had melted against him earlier.

She'd been overly tense all day. Probably from having to hand control over to her assistant. The woman was nothing if not bossy. The deejay announced the first dance: a waltz to *When You Say Nothing At All*. Tori and Garrett took the floor, and after a few minutes Ray led Lauren out to join them and pulled her into his arms.

"Close your eyes," he bade her. "It'll be over in a minute."

She glanced at him through her lashes. "You're being very nice."

"Hey, I can take a hint when it slaps me in the chest."

"I'm sorry." She laid her head on his shoulder. "I've been such a brat."

He tightened his arm around her waist. "No more than usual."

She laughed. "You're just saying that to make me feel better."

"Is it working?" He laid his cheek against the silk of her hair. "Should I brave another invitation to move indoors?"

She pulled her head back, eyed him speculatively. "To the laundry room? There are more comfortable rooms available inside, if you're truly interested in tempting me."

"Hey, I have fond memories of you in a laundry room." He kissed a path to her ear. "Remember?"

She sighed. "I remember. It wasn't one of my finest moments."

"Oh, I disagree." He twirled her and brought her back against him. "You were more than fine—you were extremely hot."

"My parents were playing poker in another room!"

"You wild child, you."

She grinned. "It *was* rather naughty."

"Excellent." Blood surged hot through his veins. "Let's go."

With her hand in his, he started off the dance floor.

"Stop." She dug her heels in. "Fun as this is..." she waved between them "...there's no future to it. I can't keep dodging into closets with you."

"Why not?"

"I'm a responsible adult. I have to think of...my reputation. Eventually someone is going to notice if we keep disappearing together."

He scowled, positive that wasn't what she'd been going to say. "Dynamite, this is Hollywood—being seen with me can only up your reputation."

"Humble, much?" She shook her head. "Seriously, whatever was between us is over."

He stood watching her walk away, appeased only slightly by the look of regret he'd seen in the depths of her eyes.

This night was never going to end. Lauren gathered empties and carried them to the tray near the bar. And turned to be confronted by the bride.

"What do you think you're doing?"

"Nothing." Lauren fought the urge to hide her hands behind her back. She waved them instead. "See? Nothing."

"Uh-huh." Tori grabbed one of her hands and drew it close as she wrapped her arm around Lauren's. "Because it's *my* day, I'll pretend I didn't see you clearing the tables."

"Forgive me. Blame it on habit."

"Only because I had to stop myself from doing the same thing twice."

"Oh, that would never do."

"That's what Garrett said."

As they neared the dance floor Lauren demanded, "Where are you taking me?"

"Here." Tori drew her right into the middle of the dancers swaying to a soft ballad. "I've danced with all my favorite people today except one. You."

Lauren's stomach jolted at the idea of swirling to music even as her heart overflowed with joy. She stepped into her sister's arms and hugged her close. If she moved slowly enough she'd be fine.

"Be happy," she whispered. "More than anything, I hope for your happiness."

"I am. Happier than I've ever been," Tori assured her. "Garrett *gets* me."

"And you get him. It's why you click."

"I want this for you." Tori's eyes glittered with happiness, with a need to share her bliss with the world. Her gaze flitted to the head table, where Garrett and his best man lounged back with a couple of beers. "Maybe you and Ray?"

"Oh, no." Lauren automatically shook her head. "Sorry to disappoint, but that's ancient history."

"Why?" Tori challenged. "Because he causes you to act spontaneously? To have a little fun? I think he's been good for you."

"Good for me?" She laughed. Oh, he did wonderful things *to* her. But good *for* her? Not by a long shot. "Think about it. He's a master manipulator."

"He's a director," Tori reminded her. "It's what he does, not who he is. He's not Brad, Lauren. He'd never hurt you."

Easy for Tori to say. Lauren would rather not risk it. Something told her Ray's power to hurt would put Brad to shame.

"Ladies, you make such a pretty picture we had to come join you." Garrett smoothly stepped between them and brought their linked hands to his mouth, where he kissed the back of Lauren's fingers before twirling her around and passing her over to Ray.

Her world spun as he moved off with Tori.

"Hey." Ray's strong arms held her steady. "Are you okay?"

"Yes. No." She leaned her forehead on his chest, prayed for her stomach to settle. No such luck. "I'm going to be sick."

Lifting her skirts, she took off at a run. And, *oh, goodness,* she wasn't going to make it. But then a hard arm curved around her back and swept her along. She reached the bathroom off the kitchen with no time to spare.

Ray held her hair while she emptied her stomach. She

was mortified—and grateful. She wanted him to go but was also glad he was there.

"I'm so sorry." She flushed and slowly lifted her head. Wait—why was she apologizing? It was *his* kid causing this inconvenience! A fact he was sure to catch on to with this display.

"No need to be. We've all had a tad too much bubbly at one point or another." He pressed a damp cloth into her hands.

She lifted it to her face, reveled in the coolness. When she lowered the cloth he held a dripping bottle of water out to her. She gratefully accepted it.

"Oh, man, I could kiss you right now."

He smiled and tucked a loose tendril behind her ear. "Sorry, Dynamite. All trips to the laundry room have been cancelled for the night."

# CHAPTER TWO

A TRILL OF BEEPS sounded from Ray's phone. And another, and another. He ignored them as he navigated the hill to his Malibu home. He'd skipped out on the post-wedding breakfast. With Garrett gone, Ray's duties were done. No need for him to linger. Nope, he was happy to put all things wedding-related behind him.

Another beep. Sounded like media alerts. He guarded his privacy, so he liked to stay on top of his media exposure. Such as it was. Better, in his opinion, to be on top of an issue than blindsided by it. With that in mind he had an assistant producer set to tell him whenever his name appeared in the news. Being best man at a major Hollywood wedding—an outdoor wedding, at that—would probably have the darn thing beeping all day long.

Once he reached his place, he dumped his garment bag at the bottom of the stairs, set his camera case on the foyer table, and wandered into the living room. He aimed the remote at his sixty-inch TV and powered it up. He'd barely tuned in to a basketball game before his phone beeped again.

He picked it up and started flipping through the alerts. Just as he'd thought, most were about the wedding. Pictures were already plastered across the internet. Distant and grainy, most gave a sense of the event but the people were unrecognizable unless you knew who they were—which would suit millions of viewers just fine.

A few obviously came from within the event. Garrett would have a fit about that.

*Ah, crud.* Just his luck—one of the up close and personal shots was of him bent over Lauren, kissing her neck. The look on her face spoke of wistful desire. So she hadn't been as indifferent as she'd pretended.

Too bad the knowledge wasn't worth the hassle it would bring. The photo had already gone viral. And, yep, right on cue his phone rang. The ringtone, an Irish ditty, announced that his grandmother waited at the other end.

"Hello, Mamó. How are you on this bright winter morning?"

"What do you know of winter? I saw on the news it's seventy degrees in Los Angeles. We've snow up to our knees. *That's* winter."

"I hope you aren't shoveling the drive again? I hired someone to keep the drive and walk clear."

"Wasted money." Annoyance flashed down the line. "We don't need it more than half the time."

"That's not the point." His brows drew together. It wasn't like Mamó to be grouchy. Thrifty, yes, but generally good-natured. He sought to distract her. "What do you have planned for your birthday?"

"Oh, they're making a fuss and I don't want it."

"They" being his aunt Ellie and his cousin Kyla.

"Nothing special about being another year older when I have nothing to show for it."

Knowing she meant great-grandkids, he dropped his head onto the back of the sofa. Lately she'd been more and more verbal about her desire for him to settle down and start a family.

"Are they taking you out to dinner?"

"No. They have a party planned at the community center. I keep telling them it's a waste of space and time."

"Everyone loves you, Mamó. I'm sure the place will be packed with your friends."

"It is difficult these days. My friends like to crow about their grandchildren and great-grandchildren. I have nothing to share."

"Mamó…"

"I know you don't want to hear this. But it is my life."

He frowned over the despair in her voice. He'd never heard her so depressed.

"I'm sorry—"

"Stop." A loud sigh blew in his ear. "Listen to me rant. Forgive an old woman her bitter babbling. I miss you, my boy. It would cheer me greatly if you could come to my party."

"A visit?" he mused. He might be able to manage that. A trip would help him to put Lauren out of his mind again.

Goodness knew there were a few harrowing memories waiting there for him. Perhaps it was time to put them behind him.

"Yes." Mamó showed a spark of life. "And you can bring your girlfriend with you."

*Uh-oh.* "Girlfriend?"

"Yes. I saw all the pictures of the two of you on the internet. You look so handsome." Her voice contained a world of excitement. "The two of you look just like a bride and groom yourselves."

In her stunning silver dress Lauren *had* looked like a bride. He remembered the stutter of his heart when she had started down the aisle toward him. In the midst of a harrowing day, she'd been the ideal distraction.

Now that played against him, giving Mamó unrealistic hopes.

"She's a lovely girl. I'm so excited to know you're seeing someone. Say you'll bring her."

This was going downhill fast. Mamó was setting herself up for disappointment if she believed a future existed for him and Lauren. "Listen—"

"You can't fool me. It's clear in the pictures you care for

her. Please, Ray?" Mamó beseeched. "You have to come and bring her with you. It's my dearest wish. And this may be my last birthday."

She was always saying things like that, but one of these days it would be true.

Comfortable in yoga pants and a cap-sleeved tee, Lauren sat on her beige sofa, feet kicked up on her ottoman coffee table, tea at her elbow, trying to focus on the mystery book she'd been saving for her vacation. Her mom, dad and brother had left for Palm Springs after breakfast, leaving Lauren free to head home and officially start her vacation.

With Tori taking two weeks off for her honeymoon, Lauren had decided to have a much needed break as well. She saw it as a great opportunity to let their new assistants take the lead on the two events scheduled for the coming week. The women had done a great job at the wedding and were ready for more responsibility.

Only a week off for Lauren, though. Hollywood's premier awards ceremony aired on Sunday, and By Arrangement was hosting Obsidian Studios' after-party.

The event represented a major goal for the company. Yes, Tori was now married to the owner, but Lauren took pride in the fact that By Arrangement had earned the contract *before* they'd got engaged. Their work for Obsidian at the Hollywood Hills Film Festival had become legendary.

For the past two months they'd been getting more work than they could handle. She'd gotten three new calls just this morning.

Much as she loved her family, Lauren had been glad to see them go. Being around her mom and not telling her about the baby had just felt wrong. But Lauren wasn't ready to confess her condition yet. Not just because she wanted Tori to be there when she revealed the news, but because Lauren needed to get used to the idea herself.

Which also explained why she wasn't ready to talk to Ray.

In a perfect world she wouldn't have to talk to Ray at all. She could dismiss him as a sperm donor and go about her life raising her child as she pleased. Unfortunately she possessed too much integrity for that option. Plus her work and his crossed paths too often for a pregnancy to go unnoticed.

A knock at the door drew her brows together in a frown. She couldn't think of a single person who might be calling. Setting her teacup on the ottoman, she made her way to the door. Where she caught sight of herself in the mirror over the hall table.

She skidded to a halt on the hardwood floor. She didn't have a lick of make-up on. After a bout of morning sickness she'd scrubbed her face clean and changed into comfy clothes. She'd barely run a brush through her hair before throwing the mass into a ponytail. She looked like a slightly hungover sixteen-year-old.

With any luck it would be a Girl Scout selling cookies. Lauren could buy a box of chocolate mints and send the child away without too much embarrassment.

A glance through the peephole proved she wasn't that lucky. Ray stood on the other side of the door. Geez, how did he even know where she lived?

Maybe if she didn't answer he'd go away. As soon as that thought registered she reached for the doorknob. It smacked of cowardice—something she refused to allow.

"Hey," Ray greeted her.

Of course he looked sensational, in black chinos and an olive lightweight knit shirt under a black leather jacket.

"Can I talk to you? It's important."

She'd bet her "important" beat his "important." But she wasn't ready to go there yet, so she really had nothing to say to him.

"I don't think that's a good idea." She blocked the door. "We pretty much said everything yesterday."

"Not this. I have a job for you."

*Uh, no.* "You'll need to call the office. I'm on vacation."

"I know." He kissed her on the temple as he pushed past her. "That makes it perfect."

Gritting her teeth, she followed him down the short hall to the open-plan living-room-kitchen combo. She had no doubt his "never take no for an answer" attitude had contributed greatly to his success as an award-winning director. On a personal front, she found it highly annoying.

"I don't think it's wise for us to work together at this time." She lingered in the opening between the hall and living area, watching as he made himself comfortable on her overstuffed couch.

"No one else will do for this particular job," he said, with such conviction it sparked her curiosity.

But she refused to be drawn in. She needed these next few days to herself, to re-evaluate and plan. To consider his part in her future.

"I'm sure that's an exaggeration."

"It's not, actually." He picked up her teacup and sniffed; he took a sip and nodded. "My grandmother's birthday is this week." He went to the kitchen and began opening cupboards until he found a mug. "I talked to her this morning. I've never heard her sound so down. All her friends are great-grandmothers and she's pouting because she doesn't have a baby to dandle on her knee."

"I'm sorry to hear that." Lauren took the mug from him and set it on the counter. "What does that have to do with me?"

"She asked me to come to her party. I'm hoping if I go it will cheer her up."

"Good luck with that." She did wish him luck, knowing how stubborn *her* grandmother could be when stuck on that topic. "I still don't see how By Arrangement can be of assistance. We have no connections in New York. If we'd had more warning we could have put something together for you, but at this late date—"

"I don't need your expertise as an event coordinator," he broke in. "I need a date."

She blinked at him; let her mind catch up with his words. "You want me to go to New York with you?"

"Yes. We leave tomorrow morning. I've already arranged the flight."

Of course he had. She pointed toward the door. "Get out."

"Lauren, I'm serious. I need your help."

"You're insane if you think I'm going to New York with you."

"I don't expect you to drop everything for nothing." He treated her to his charming smile. "I want to hire you."

The attempt at manipulation and the reminder that his request was a job offer only made the whole thing worse. Fortunately it had the benefit of reminding her he was a client and as such deserved a respectful response.

Drawing on her professional persona, she breathed deep, seeking calm. "As I already mentioned, I'm on vacation."

"Name your price." He would not be deterred. "I need you. Mamó saw that tabloid picture of us a couple of months ago, and now all the internet pictures of us at the wedding, and is excited about the idea of me having a girlfriend. All she wants for her birthday is for me to bring you with me."

"I'm not comfortable with the idea of deceiving your grandmother. If that's what you're looking for I'm sure there are any number of actresses who would be pleased to help you."

"It's not like that." He scowled. "It has to be you because you're the one in the pictures and because we do have a relationship."

"Did." She corrected him. "We had a fling." Calling

their frantic rendezvous a relationship seemed a stretch. "It's over."

He stepped closer, played with the ends of her ponytail. "It doesn't have to be. We could have fun on this trip."

Gazing into his cheerful blue eyes, she experienced the irrational desire to lunge for what he offered. She didn't think when she was in his arms—she just felt. An option that held huge appeal when her mind still whirled from the fact she was expecting his baby.

"No." She spun out of his reach, crossed her arms in front of her—protecting herself, protecting their child. "We couldn't. I told you, there's no future for us. I like to be in the driver's seat and so do you."

"I don't mind riding shotgun to a beautiful woman on occasion."

"Liar."

He laughed. "Okay, you got me. But we manage okay. What's wrong with having a little fun?"

"It's not me." Which was true—even if there wasn't a child to consider. "And I'm too busy. Don't forget the awards are this weekend. We're handling the Obsidian party."

"But you're on vacation. And we'll be back by Saturday."

"I prefer to be available in case the new assistants need help. And, believe me, I have things to keep me occupied." Like planning a new future. Making an actual doctor's appointment. Strategizing how she was going to handle him.

Ray stepped back, propped his hands on his hips. He appeared truly perplexed by her refusal. "Lauren, it's my *grandmother.*"

Okay, he knew what button to push. She didn't wish his grandmother ill. She actually admired his attempt to help the older woman. But she couldn't let her sympathy lead her down a dangerous path.

"I'm sorry. She's going to have to make do with you."

"Right." His blue eyes turned cold. He turned away. "Sorry to have bothered you."

She closed her eyes rather than watch him walk away. A moment later she heard the front door close behind him.

Lauren's conscience niggled her all morning and into the afternoon. For all his forceful charm and pre-planning ways, Ray had genuinely been concerned for his grandmother.

And, though they were no longer and never really had been seeing each other, the tabloid and internet pictures gave the appearance they had. Ray's penchant for privacy—well known in Hollywood and no doubt by his family—only added credibility to his grandmother's assumption.

But every time she considered changing her mind her heart raced and she remembered how insane his proposal was. If she agreed to go with him she'd be the unbalanced one. The man rode roughshod over everyone. Case in point: he had bought her airline ticket without even getting her agreement first.

So arrogant, so controlling… She shuddered. So not a good combination.

Except her life was now irrevocably linked to his. The trip to New York would present the perfect opportunity to see Ray in the midst of his family. What better way to learn what family meant to him? His concern for his grandmother was already an eye-opener. How could she refuse to help him and then expect to have a harmonious relationship going forward?

Simple—she couldn't.

A child grew within her. Ray's child. Mamó's great-grandchild. Which meant Lauren had no choice but to go to New York.

She consoled herself with the knowledge that the trip

would provide the perfect opportunity to tell him the news of their pending parenthood.

She hated making spur-of-the-moment decisions. She liked to plan, set goals, make lists. Order prevented chaos, allowed her to be prepared, in control. She hadn't reached that point when it came to the baby. Or Ray.

If she was going to go to New York with him she wanted to lay down some ground rules.

Mind made up, she changed and drove to Ray's hillside home in Malibu. It took close to an hour. She pulled in to his flagstone driveway and parked. He lived alone except for the middle-aged couple who took care of the house and gardens. Fred and Ethel lived in a small villa on the grounds.

Lauren smirked as always at the couple's names. They were poignant reminders of home. You didn't grow up in Palm Springs, rich with old Hollywood history, without being familiar with *I Love Lucy.*

She rang the doorbell, listened to it echo through the house. Given the size of the place, she gave it a few minutes before ringing again. Ray's home took up four acres and consisted of five buildings: the four-thousand-square-foot main house, a multi-level garage with a heliport on top, a guest house, a pool house, and the caretakers' villa. The grounds were terraced and included a tennis/basketball court, a pool, and two spas.

He also had top-of-the-line security with high-end electronic capabilities. Ray loved his gadgets. She didn't look into the camera above the door, but she knew it was there.

She frowned and glanced at her watch. Maybe he was out. But if that were the case why had she been let in the front gate? Lauren had allowed plenty of time for someone to respond to the bell, which meant he was here and making her wait or he was refusing to acknowledge her.

*Now* who was the coward?

"What do you want?" His disembodied voice came from no discernible source.

"To talk to you," she replied, keeping her gaze fixed on the ground. If he wanted to see her face he needed to open the door.

"I believe it was made clear there was nothing further to discuss between the two of us."

She crossed her arms over her chest. This was why they weren't compatible—the constant play for power. "I'm not having a conversation through a door."

"What?" he mocked her. "Am I lacking graciousness as a host?"

"Fine." She turned on her peep-toed heels. "Forget it."

All the better for her. No awkward acting required in New York, and she'd made the attempt, so he couldn't hold her earlier rejection against her.

The door opened at her back and a strong male hand wrapped around her upper arm. "Please come in." He led her inside to the large, open living room. "I wouldn't want you to come all this way and not state your business."

She walked past him and took a seat on an oval suede sofa in rich beige. *Shoot*, an already difficult discussion had just got harder. Because he looked yummy. He wore the same pants and shirt he'd had on earlier, but he was sexily disheveled, with his sandy hair mussed up, the start of a five o'clock shadow, and bare feet.

When she didn't answer he dropped into a chair across from her, knees spread, arms braced on muscular thighs.

She swallowed hard.

"No door, Dynamite." He gave her his full attention. "What do you want? If you'll remember, I have some packing to do."

Seeking composure, she straightened her shoulders and crossed her hands over her purse in her lap. "I've reconsidered my earlier decision. I'm willing to help you with your grandmother."

He considered her for a moment, his blue eyes assessing. "What's it going to cost me?"

Annoyed at the mention of payment, she seared him with a glare.

"By Arrangement is an event-oriented business. We do not get involved in family dynamics. I would be doing this as a favor for a friend."

Okay, that was stretching it. She'd be doing it to get to know her child's father better.

"So now we're friends?" He lifted one brown eyebrow.

She shrugged. She'd like to think they could be friends, but the chemistry between them made the ease of friendship a difficult prospect.

"The point is I'm willing to help. And it's not going to cost you anything more than a few common courtesies."

His eyes narrowed. "I knew there'd be something."

"Just a few ground rules so we don't get tripped up."

He sat back. "Such as?"

"Well, to start with I think we need to be as truthful as possible."

"Agreed."

"It'll be less complicated. And I prefer to be as honest as we can."

"No argument. What's next?"

"I want separate bedrooms."

He cocked his head. "It's my grandmother. I'm pretty sure that's guaranteed."

She relaxed a little. So far, so good. "No fostering false hope that our relationship will mature to the next level."

"'Mature to the next level?'" he repeated. "Who talks that way?"

"Nice." Her shoulders went back. "You know what I mean."

"Don't get her hopes up that we'll get married." He frowned over the words. "You really don't have to worry about that."

"I'm not expecting a proposal." A long-suffering sigh lifted her breasts, drawing his attention downward. How predictable. "I want you to promise you won't let concern for your grandmother sway you into implying something you can't deliver. She'll only be hurt in the long run."

"You can be assured I'm not going to do anything to hurt Mamó."

*Uh-huh.* She believed his love and concern were genuine. But she also knew his penchant for control, and that he had a compulsive need to fix things. She easily saw one emotion feeding into the other.

"The last is no unnecessary touching."

He threw back his head and laughed. "You've got to be kidding. The point is that we're a *couple*. How do we portray intimacy without touching?"

She understood his confusion. The man was very tactile —he couldn't *not* touch…things, materials, people.

"I didn't say no touching. Of course there will need to be public displays of affection. But you're a master director, brilliant at evoking emotion. I'm sure you can manage with the minimum of physical contact."

"So PDAs are okay?" His gaze ran over her as his mind connected the dots. He was to keep his hands to himself in private. "So businesslike. I thought you were doing this as a friendly gesture. Why so strict?"

How to answer that? The baby motivated her to help him, because she needed to maintain a position of power. But that wasn't the only reason. Before she'd known about the baby she'd fought her desires because they turned her into someone she wasn't. Reckless, abandoned, acquiescent.

She'd subjugated her will to a man once before. It had changed who she was—a mistake she'd never make again.

She considered telling him about the baby—just putting it out there. But, no. He was already dealing with a distressed grandmother. It wouldn't be fair to drop the baby news on him, too.

"I've put what was between us behind me. Yet there's no denying the sexual chemistry between us." She gave him the lesser truth. "I don't want to jeopardize the progress I've made. This is a deal-breaker, Ray."

"Okay, you win." He threw his hands up in surrender. "I promise to keep my hands to myself."

She knew she'd have to remind him of his pledge, but it would do for now.

"When is our flight?"

The limousine pulled to a stop in front of Lauren's home and Ray stepped out. He knew she co-owned the bunga-low-style duplex along with her sister. The arrangement allowed the twins the proximity they enjoyed, yet gave each of them their privacy. Perfect for sisters who were both friends and partners, or so she'd told him.

Of course that would all change now Tori had married Garrett. Would the twins keep the property and rent out Tori's side? Or would they sell, leaving Lauren to find a new home?

In a flash he saw her at his place, bringing order to his chaos, watching daily edits with him in the media room, claiming the gaming loft as her home office.

He froze with his hand poised to knock.

His head shook along with a full-body shudder. Must be residual fallout from the wedding. His overactive imagination tweaking on domestic bliss overload.

He knocked. He still puzzled over why Lauren had changed her mind and agreed to accompany him to New York. Nothing really made sense except that family mattered to her.

He'd seen that first-hand last Thanksgiving, when he'd learned that Garrett was spending the day alone, with nothing to occupy him but memories of his father's passing and the shattering of his own body in a car accident the previous year.

Of course Ray had invited his buddy over for Thanksgiving dinner, and then made an emergency call to Lauren to see if By Arrangement could pull off a miracle.

She'd been about to sit down to dinner with her family, but had named a couple of restaurants he could try. He'd cut her off to invite her family to join him and Garrett. The home-cooked deal had appealed to Ray, and additional people would help to distract Garrett.

And, of course, thinking of Thanksgiving brought back memories of their laundry room tryst.

Luckily the front door opened, keeping him from remembering the details of their heated session on the washing machine.

"Good morning." Lauren came out, pulling a small suitcase. "Can you grab the garment bag?" She motioned to the blue bag hanging over the hall closet.

He stepped inside and grabbed it. "Just the two bags?"

"You don't have to be sarcastic." She glanced at her luggage with a frown. "I know it's a lot for a week, but you didn't mention anything except your grandmother's birthday so I have to be prepared for anything."

"I wasn't being sarcastic." He handed her bag to the driver, who also took the roller bag, then held the back door for her. "If you're prepared for anything I'm surprised you don't have twice as many bags."

She gave a small smile and slid across the seat. Her jacket dragged on the seat behind her and he swept it out of the way as he slid in after her.

"Is this your heaviest jacket?" He fingered the fleece-lined raincoat. "The forecast in Queens is for snow."

"I'm sure it'll be fine." She pulled the fabric free and tossed the coat over her purse on the other side of her.

"Fine for Southern California is not the same as fine for New York. You'll freeze if that's all you take." The car pulled away from the curb. "I'll have the driver swing by Rodeo Drive."

He reached for the intercom. Her hand intercepted his, pushing it down.

"Forget it. I'm not buying a coat I'll only wear for a week."

She quickly retracted her touch. The woman did like her rules.

"I brought sweaters and a warm scarf. I'll be fine."

He snorted. "Let me know when you change your mind."

She glanced at him over her shoulder. "Why? So you can say, *I told you so*?"

"So I can take you shopping." He trained his gaze on the muted TV monitor across the way. "The *I told you so* will be strictly implied."

Out of the corner of his eye he caught her grin. He relaxed back into his seat. The trip might not be the total cluster bash he feared.

"Please. Hold your breath," she advised, all sweetness and light.

He turned to address her sass, only to stop when she pressed a hand to her stomach. A glance at her face revealed she'd lost all the color in her cheeks. Concern tightened his chest.

"Lauren, what is it?"

She sat very still, slowly drawing in a deep breath. "I wasn't ready for that last turn. It sent my stomach spinning."

"What can I do?"

"Can you lower the partition?" She swallowed repeatedly. "I think it will help if I can see where we're going."

He picked up the remote and did as she'd asked. The additional light showed her color was returning. "If you're not feeling well we can delay our flight for a day."

"That won't be necessary." She dug in her purse and

pulled out a dry protein bar. "I should have eaten something earlier. I'll be all right once I have a couple of bites." She looked at him oddly. "You're awfully cavalier about our departure time."

"It's not a commercial flight. I called a friend and he's agreed to lend me his jet. Barring emergencies, it's at my disposal for the next week."

"Must be nice." She closed her eyes and leaned her head back as she chewed. Her hand lingered over her stomach.

"Rest." He ran a knuckle down her cheek. "I'll let you know when we get to the airport."

Instead of flinching away, she leaned into his touch. After another sweep of her silky skin he left her to rest. He took heart from the exchange. If she could take comfort from him, the connection between them wasn't entirely extinguished.

Strong enough, he hoped, to convince his family for a week.

And maybe to allow for one more hook-up?

Because Lauren might see them as over, but he wasn't doing well with the whole cold turkey approach. He watched the soft rise and fall of her breasts and struggled with the desire to pull her into his arms.

No, his feelings about their relationship didn't match hers at all. Sure, he believed in keeping things short and light, but *he* usually called the where and when.

And when he looked at her he saw unfinished business.

# CHAPTER THREE

LAUREN ACCEPTED RAY'S suggestion to rest as an opportunity to avoid conversation for the rest of their trip to the airport. She shrugged out of the brown cropped jacket she wore over a cream sweater and jeans, then settled back against the seat and watched the road through the veil of her lashes.

Thank goodness seeing where they were headed had helped to calm her queasy stomach.

One thing was for certain. She needed to get this morning sickness under control or she'd be making explanations before she was ready. Ray was too intelligent not to put the pieces together with them living in each other's pockets.

And then there was his grandmother, aunt and cousin. Hopefully they'd be too caught up in Ray's visit and Mamó's birthday to pay much attention to her.

At the airport they departed from the commuter terminal. Expedited VIP service streamlined their boarding process and within minutes she climbed the steps to a mid-sized jet. The scent of fine leather hit her as soon as she entered the plane. Fortunately the baby had no objection to the smell.

Lauren made her way down the aisle between half a dozen armchair-style seats in creamy beige. The second half of the cabin contained two face-to-face couches of the same color in a soft ultra-suede fabric. At the end a door stood open on a full-sized restroom.

Just *wow*. This was totally going to spoil her for flying coach.

Pretending a sophistication she didn't feel, she turned to Ray. "Where do I sit?"

"Wherever you want." He indicated two armchairs facing each other. "Why don't we start here? I asked the attendant to bring you some tea once we're in the air. She'll also bring you something to eat. Do you want eggs and bacon? Bagels or muffins? Fruit?"

"I don't care for anything right now." She sank into the chair next to the window.

"A few bites of protein bar aren't much," he protested. "You need something more."

"Welcome aboard." The attendant, an attractive brunette in a gray pantsuit, appeared at her elbow. "My name is Julie. I'll be serving you today. If you need anything you can call me via the remote, or just push this button." She showed Lauren on her armrest. "I'll bring tea when we've reached cruising altitude. What more would you like?"

"Nothing for—"

"Thank you, Julie." Ray cut Lauren off. "Please bring a selection of bagels, fruit, and yogurt."

Lauren slammed him with a glare at his arrogant disregard for her wishes. She should know if she was hungry.

"May I take your things?" Julie offered. "There's a closet at the front of the cabin. You'll have full access during the flight."

Lauren handed off her purse and coat. She waited until the other woman had disappeared before addressing Ray.

"If you hope to get along on this trip you will refrain from treating me like a child."

"Then don't behave like one."

His gaze roved over her. She felt the weight of it everywhere it touched.

"You're still pale. Food helped in the car. I can only

assume it would be better if you had something more. It would please me if you ate. But the choice is yours."

She gritted her teeth. To argue further would only make her sound petty.

Luckily the pilot's voice filled the cabin. "Please fasten your seatbelts. We'll be departing momentarily."

Avoiding Ray's gaze, she glanced out the window as the plane began to move. His reasonableness did nothing to appease her. In fact it only annoyed her, putting her in the position of being unreasonable—an intolerable situation, which was totally his fault.

It would please him if she ate? Seriously?

Right this minute she felt fine. She hoped to stay that way through takeoff. And the thought of food...? Not helping.

As a view of the airport, planes, and air traffic personnel flowed by the porthole window she marveled once again at her current circumstances. The only explanation she could come up with was she must have royally ticked off Lady Karma in another life, because she should not be pregnant.

She'd started on the pill. Ray had worn condoms. Yeah, they'd been frantic for each other, but they'd also been responsible. Okay, there had been that once when the condom broke. Yet—hello?—still on the pill. Sure, her doctor had warned her that it took time for the body to adjust, but it had been a month. Well, almost.

The force of takeoff pushed her back in her seat as the plane began to rise. Her fingers curled into fists on the armrests, her nails digging into the soft leather. She closed her eyes, willed her stomach to behave.

"Are you okay?"

Ray's voice sounded next to her ear at the same time as a warm hand settled over her clenched fingers.

Her eyes flew open. When had he moved next to her?

More to the point, when had his touch become an instant soother?

It had to be the distraction, her logical mind asserted, but she didn't care. She turned her hand over, threaded her fingers through his and accepted the warmth and comfort he freely offered.

Tension eased away, taking the rising nausea with it.

"Thank you." She gave him a feeble smile.

"Nervous flyer?" he sympathized.

"Mmm…" She made a noncommittal sound. Poor guy. Her hormones were all over the place, her emotions likewise. Talk about mixed signals. *She* didn't know how she felt—how could he begin to guess?

"Not usually." She made an effort to participate in the conversation, hoping the resulting distraction would continue to work on her mind and stomach. "I guess I'm nervous about the whole trip. We haven't truly discussed how we're going to handle things. I'm not comfortable lying to your grandmother."

"Me neither," he said. "So we don't lie."

Eying his stoic expression, she felt the muscles in her shoulders begin to tense again. "If you're suggesting—"

"I'm not." He squeezed her fingers. "We're friends. At least I hope you consider me a friend. That's what we put out there."

Because his touch felt too good, she pulled her hand free of his. On another level she noticed the plane had leveled out. "But everyone has an expectation there's more between us."

"Exactly. We'll just be ourselves and they'll see what they want to see."

She tapped her fingers on the armrest as she considered his approach. "Still seems a little artificial."

"The power of illusion comes from a collective awareness. People believe what they want to believe. Directors use viewer expectations as a tool to manipulate the audience's emotions all the time. It doesn't make what they feel any less real."

"Do you hear the words you're using? *Manipulate... audience.* This is your family we're talking about, not a theater full of moviegoers."

She understood the concept he presented, and, yes, she expected it would work as well as he stated. The truth worked for her. Leaving his family with preconceived notions that went well beyond reality was more iffy.

"Look." His gaze earnest, he picked up her hand, swept his thumb over the pulse at her wrist. "I know the girlfriend front isn't ideal. Ordinarily I wouldn't even consider it. But you have no idea how upset my grandmother sounded." Concern darkened his eyes to a soft azure. "If this plan lifts her spirits, it's worth a little discomfort on my part."

"Okay," she agreed. And again removed her hand from under his. Bottom line: his concern was genuine. And, if she were honest, it wasn't as if she and Tori hadn't occasionally manufactured events to gain their mother's cooperation to get something they wanted.

His family—his call. She'd agreed to come, so she'd do as he wished.

"Teatime."

Julie had arrived with a cart. She reached past them to pull a table from a wall slot, trapping Lauren next to Ray. The sudden intimacy suffocated her. She wanted to protest. Of course she didn't.

She was too strong to give in to weakness, too smart to reveal it to the opposition.

Onto the table Julie slid a tray, artfully displaying an array of bagels, both toasted and non-toasted, along with a healthy heaping of cream cheese, butter, and jellies. There were containers of yogurt and a lovely selection of fresh fruit. Next came steaming pots of hot water and a small basket of teas.

A midsized plate and linen-wrapped silverware were

placed in front of each of them. "May I serve you?" Julie asked.

"We'll help ourselves, thank you." Ray's charming smile caused the poised woman to blush.

"Please buzz me if you require anything more," she bade them, and then disappeared to her niche in the front of the plane.

Lauren waited for her stomach to revolt. When it didn't she reached for the basket of teas, chose a soothing decaffeinated blend and steeped it in one of the pots. When it looked the right color, she poured the brew into a delicate teacup.

Ray slathered cream cheese on a cinnamon bagel and slid melon, pineapple chunks and a few blackberries on his plate.

"Can I fix you anything?" he asked, after she'd taken her first sip.

"Perhaps half a plain bagel, with a light spread of cream cheese."

He nodded and a moment later placed it on her plate. She cut it into quarters and picked up a corner to nibble on.

"You know, I'm all for sticking to the truth and all..." She set her cup back in its saucer. "But the details are still going to be a bit sketchy. You do realize we've never been on an actual date?" She stabbed at a plump berry on his plate and ate it.

His eyes narrowed in thought. He reached for a carton of peach yogurt, opened it and scooped in a few berries. He took a couple of bites before pointing his spoon at her.

"We've kept a low profile."

Her brows lifted. "You're a little too good at this."

He grinned and offered her the yogurt carton. "I'm a director. It's my job to invent and interpret."

"Convenient." Not even thinking about it, she accepted the yogurt.

The flavors, peach and blackberry, exploded in her

mouth. A few more bites finished it off. She sighed. A glance at her plate revealed he'd gotten his wish. She'd eaten all her bagel plus fruit and his yogurt. And she felt great. More energized than she had in forever.

"Finally you've a little color in your cheeks."

She gave him a cool glance. "Saying *I told you so* is unbecoming."

He shook his sandy head. "I'm just glad you're feeling better."

"Thanks." What else could she say without sounding petty? To his credit, he appeared sincere.

To break the moment she pushed the button on her armrest. Julie appeared within moments to clear the table. But all too soon she and Ray were alone again. It was all she could do not to twitch in her seat. How to get him to move away?

Turned out she didn't have to do anything. Phone in hand, he stood up.

"If you'll excuse me, I have some calls to make?"

She nodded and he moved across the aisle and up to another row of seats. Able to breathe freely, she refused to acknowledge she missed the heat and comfort of his proximity. Some alone time to think was exactly what she needed. She felt the best she had in days—make that weeks.

Maybe she'd actually be able to concentrate and come up with a course of action for this abrupt change in her carefully crafted life plan. So far she hadn't quite been able to wrap her mind around the enormity of the fact she carried a child within her. And that kept her from making sense out of the chaos in her head.

Which left her feeling out of control and desperate to get her life back.

Panicked, really.

The last time she'd given up control, she'd lost a part of her soul.

Lauren couldn't go through that again—especially

when she had a child to think of. She required her lists, her goals, her plans. She craved order, needed to be in charge. Only then could she cope.

She stared unseeing out the window.

Some things were obvious. Once Tori returned Lauren would tell her family. She would continue to work. She would tell Ray. It all sounded simple and straightforward. It couldn't be more complex.

Even telling her family. Sure, they would love and support her. She had no doubt of that. But there'd also be disappointment and concern. And questions. Personal questions, not easy to answer.

Continuing to work would require compromise and sacrifice. Deciding between daycare and a nanny was only one decision to be made requiring careful research. She also needed to consider housing—whether to sell the duplex and move to a bigger place in a family-friendly area. It didn't need to be done now, but it was already on her mind. A part of the mix keeping her from finding the necessary peace to deal with everything.

Telling Ray. Yeah, she'd been playing ostrich there. She knew she had to give him the news. Yet the where and when were still questions. She had no idea how to approach him, but she did know it wouldn't be before this deal with his grandmother played out.

It wouldn't be fair to distract him at this time.

And, truly, everything else hinged on his reaction. Any plans she conceived were contingent on how involved he'd want to be.

Her stomach roiled. The realization threatened the scant control she'd managed to muster.

She drew out her phone and powered it up. She had a couple of her own calls to make.

About forty minutes before they were scheduled to land Ray roused Lauren. Halfway through the trip she'd

stretched out on one of the couches and slid into a solid
sleep. She hadn't moved an eyelash when he'd dropped a
blanket over her and stuffed a pillow under her head.

She was slow to awaken. He had no idea if that was
natural or not, as they'd never actually slept together. He
tended not to sleep with the women in his life. Too messy.

How fragile she looked. He traced the shadows under
the fan of her lashes. She said she wasn't sick, yet she was
tired and pale and a couple of times he'd caught an expression on her face that made him think she might be fighting off nausea. Perhaps it was the aftereffects of stress.
Handling her sister's wedding during Hollywood's biggest party season must have been a challenge, even for a
pro like her.

She was such a strong woman—quick and intelligent
and in control—he tended to overlook the fact she was
quite delicate.

"Lauren." He ran his hand up her arm, gave her shoulder a gentle shake. "Wake up, Sleeping Beauty."

"Hmm?" She sighed and shifted onto her side. "Ga-
way."

He grinned. "No, I'm not going away." Leaning over
her, he pressed his lips to hers. "But I'll join you if you'd
like." That ought to wake her up.

"Ray..." Her lips opened under his and an arm snaked
around his neck, pulling him close.

The action put him off balance. He went down on one
knee to keep from tumbling on top of her. He'd happily
follow up on his offer to join her on the couch as soon as
he knew her mind was as engaged as her body.

Meantime, he sank into the kiss.

Instantly the chemistry ignited between them. Angling
his head, he slid his tongue past her lips to taste the honey
of her mouth. Her sleepy response seduced him into a slow,
deep exploration. The meandering journey pulled them

down a path not yet taken. The softness of the moment was different but every bit as hot as their bolder encounters.

She sighed and shifted fully onto her back. The drag of her fingers through his hair was a dreamy caress, a subtle demand for more, for longer, for slow and sensual. He willingly set the pace, lingering over each touch, each taste, each smell, satiating all his senses. Her breath sighed over his cheek and he took satisfaction in each little moue and gasp.

Never had he burned for a woman like he did for her. And she was right there with him, her responsiveness inspiring him to new depths.

The gradual, sultry building of passion urged him to tenderness, to lengthy kisses and gentle insistence. He worked his hand under her sweater and glided up her silky skin, seeking the bounty of her breast.

She suddenly went very still and her hand came down on his, effectively pushing the stop button on his attempt to move their embrace to the next step.

"Not a good idea," she mumbled in a sleep-husky voice.

He groaned and tested her resolve, sweeping his thumb across the warm flesh of her stomach. She gasped and tightened her hold, but the knit of her sweater separating her grasp from his was a thin barrier to his persistence.

"Shh, Dynamite," he whispered against her lips, "you're dreaming."

"Liar." Her lips lifted in a smile under his and then she turned her head aside. "My body is too alive for me to be asleep." She pulled his hand free of her clothes. "We agreed no touching."

"You started it, wrapping yourself all around me." He kissed a path up her jawline to whisper in her ear. "Let me finish it. We can start the no touching when we get to New York."

She moaned deep in her throat—a sound he took to

mean she was tempted, if the look in her golden eyes meant anything.

"Uh-uh." She planted both hands on his chest and pushed. "I did not start it. You kissed me first. When I had no resistance. Unfair, Ray."

He let her up, slid onto the couch next to her when she pushed into a sitting position. "Spoilsport."

An arch glare came his way. "Really?"

The show of ire along with her mussed hair and just-kissed lips was too sexy for words. Made him want to take up where they had left off. Forget about apologizing. Besides, he still maintained she'd started it. His had been a mere peck on the lips; she had taken it to the next level.

Not waiting for a response, she rolled her eyes, then glanced back at him. "Why did you wake me?"

He checked his watch—much safer than contemplating her. "In ten minutes we begin our descent. I thought you'd like to freshen up before we buckle up."

"Oh. I would, thanks." She made her escape.

While she did her thing he went through his email and texts. The car service he used in New York advised that a driver was waiting. His meeting with the mayor was confirmed. And Mamó couldn't wait to see him.

With a sigh he slipped the phone into his pocket. This trip was long overdue. Sure, he saw his family regularly, stopping off in New York or flying them to him two or three times a year. But he rarely went back to the old neighborhood. Certainly not for any length of time. Too many memories he'd rather not deal with.

Lauren came back, looking as calm and fresh as when she'd first boarded the plane. Something he envied, considering he still ached from their recent bout of passion. He earned another glare when he settled in the seat next to hers, and those luscious lips opened ready to protest, but the pilot came on, demanding they buckle up.

The landing went well and soon Ray saw Lauren seated

into a sleek black town car. She promptly slid to the far side of the bench seat, leaving at least a foot between them, and pulled out her tablet, effectively shutting him out. Within a few minutes they were swallowed by the late-afternoon traffic headed through the borough of Queens to Queens Village.

His grandmother lived in a two-family, two-story pitched-roof house on a postage-stamp-sized lot. He'd tried to upgrade her to a bigger house on a larger lot in a better area, but she refused to move. She'd lived in her house since she'd moved in as a bride and intended to stay until the day she died. Rather than argue, he'd paid off the mortgage, bought out the neighbors so his aunt could move in, and made sure the house remained sound and safe.

"We're here," he said as the pale gray building with its white filigree fence came into view.

Lauren leaned close to look out the window. "Quaint house."

He explained his attempt to relocate her. "I told you she was stubborn."

Cars overflowed the driveway and street, forcing the driver to double park. Ray stepped out and turned to help Lauren. Leaving the driver to bring their bags, Ray threaded their fingers together, more for his benefit than hers, and climbed the brick stairs to the front door. It flew open before his knuckles connected with the wood.

"Ray!" Aunt Ellie pushed open the screen and pulled him into a big hug. "It's so good to see you. Come inside." She stepped back, dragging him with her, and by extension Lauren. "Everyone—Ray is here."

Pandemonium broke out. Women of all ages launched themselves at him. He barely recognized most of them but he hugged them anyway, one-armed. Because he was not letting go of Lauren. Behind him he heard her fielding greetings.

"Hello."

"Hi."

"Nice to meet you."

"I'm Lauren."

These were his grandmother's, aunt's, cousin's friends. He got that they were proud of him and wanted to show off. So he smiled and nodded and forged ahead.

He froze when he spied Mrs. Renwicki. The smug look on her face reminded him of her granddaughter, Camilla. And, *bang*, the past was right in his face.

Turning his back on it, he finally broke through the crowd of people and furniture, and there was Mamó. Short and plump, her white-gray hair woven into a braid and pinned in a bun on top of her head, just as he always pictured her. She rose from her floral wingback chair and framed his face in her wrinkled hands.

"Ray, my boy, I'm so happy to see you." She kissed him on the cheek.

"Mamó, you look great." He gave her a full-on hug. "I've missed you."

"Then you should visit more often." She admonished him. "But you're here now, and you've brought the beautiful Lauren with you."

"Yes." He met Lauren's guarded gaze as he wrapped his arm around her waist and drew her forward. She was a trouper for putting up with this gauntlet. "Thanks," he whispered before turning to his grandmother. "Mamó, this is—"

"This is Lauren!" Mamó broke in, taking Lauren's hands in both of hers. "Your fiancée."

# CHAPTER FOUR

LAUREN BLINKED AT Ray's grandmother, the word *fiancée* echoing through the room. Or was it just through her head?

"Oh…" Lauren's smile froze in place while her mind scrambled for an appropriate response. Did she carelessly laugh it off, politely deny the allegation, or go along with the crazy suggestion?

This broke so many of her rules. What was Ray thinking? Was the tight grip on her elbow warning or encouragement?

She angled her head up and around, her gaze meeting his. The shock in his eyes reassured her that his surprise matched hers.

"Mamó—" he began, and Lauren sighed, willing to let him handle the unexpected claim. "We're not—"

"Forgive me," Mamó rushed in, cutting him off. She kissed Lauren's cheek, color high in her cheeks and a look of pleading in her pale blue eyes. "I know you wanted it to be a surprise, but I couldn't resist sharing the news with my closest friends." Her gaze flitted to an older woman across the room before lifting to meet her grandson's eyes. "Please say it's all right."

Behind her, Lauren felt Ray's chest expand in a heavy sigh. "Mamó, I don't know where you got your information, but—"

The hands holding hers shook as the older woman nearly crushed Lauren's fingers.

"Of *course* we forgive you," Lauren rushed to say. It was good to know Ray would uphold his promise to her, but she couldn't let him embarrass his grandmother in front of all her friends.

The way he suddenly relaxed told her it had been a difficult decision.

"Thank you," Mamó breathed in Lauren's ear as she hugged her.

A chorus of congratulations rang out and a few people rushed at them to offer a new round of hearty handshakes and some hugs.

Ray handled it like a pro, reminding Lauren of his short stint as an actor before he'd moved behind the camera.

"I want to see the ring," Kyla demanded, pushing to the front. She grabbed Lauren's hand, only to frown at her naked ring finger. Kyla turned the look on her cousin. "Where's the ring, cuz? I expected to see at least a couple of carats."

"We thought we'd ring-shop while we're in town."

Oh, he was good. He handled the crowd of women like a pro. He charmed them all. He was attentive, a little flirtatious, and slippery as an eel. But Lauren didn't relax. There were too many questions, too many people, too many opportunities to mess up.

"Food's ready," Ellie called out.

Lauren hid a grimace, the thought of food too much, but her stomach growled. She placed a hand on her belly, trying to decipher her body's mixed signals as the rest of the guests eagerly moved into the dining room.

"You okay?"

Ray appeared in front of her. It was the first moment they'd had alone since walking through the door.

"Listen, I'm sorry about the whole engagement thing. Especially after I promised nothing like this would happen. I'll talk to Mamó and see if we can't get it all straightened out."

Lauren shook her head. "I think it's too late for that."

"Yeah," he agreed, a frown pulling his golden-brown brows together. "She got herself into a pickle. Thanks for not embarrassing her."

"Of course." She sent him an arch glance. "She obviously wants to see you settled down."

"And bouncing a baby or two on her lap," he bit out. "It's no excuse for putting us in this position."

Mention of a baby put a tremble in her muscles. She locked her knees and tried for practical. "We knew she was hopeful of a deeper relationship when we headed east," she reminded him. "If we stick to our rules we'll be fine."

"I'm glad you're taking this so well." He placed a hand in the small of her back and directed her toward a table laden with food. "You can still expect an apology."

She sighed, seeing his persistence as a need to control the situation. But she also respected his desire to honor his promise and protect her. Then she reached the food table and all thought left her head as hunger took over.

Grabbing a plate, she filled it with salads, fruit, and meat. She reached for a roll as Ray handed her napkin-wrapped utensils.

"Good to see you have your appetite back." He kissed her on the top of her head.

Okay, she could take that as patronizing or affectionate—neither of which suited her. Deciding to ignore him, she took her plate and found a single seat next to his cousin Kyla. He frowned at her choice and ate standing up near the mantel.

Lauren smiled around a bite of potato salad and listened to the surrounding women talk about tomorrow's party. They were excited because there'd be dancing, but a comment about lack of partners had Lauren glancing around the room. Many of these same people would be guests at the party, and the ratio hit at about three women to each man. Hmm, maybe she could help with that.

A tall, gray-haired gentleman with a dignified bearing hovered around Mamó. A flare of awareness tingled through Lauren, signaling a connection between them. Interesting… Must be a strong link. She rarely experienced the matchmaking sensation without Tori nearby to bolster their shared talent.

The topic moved on to where she should shop for her wedding rings. She stiffened for a moment, then gave a mental shrug. What the heck? She could get behind a fictitious shopping trip.

Thirty minutes later Ray was standing chatting with Mamó's neighbor when Mrs. Renwicki joined them. She gushed over his engagement.

"I'm *so* happy you've finally put Camilla behind you."

Mamó's neighbor nodded and patted his arm as the other woman went on.

"My granddaughter is happily married, expecting her third child. It's time you found some happiness too."

The woman had some nerve, throwing Camilla in his face. He wondered if she knew of the great-grandchild her precious girl had thrown away. Having nothing to say to her, he excused himself and walked away.

The confrontation confirmed his worst fears. His most humiliating moment remained fresh in the minds of the community that had borne witness to it.

His faithful friend was at the ready, and he lifted the camera to his eye and took a few shots. He sought out Lauren with the lens. Seeing her soothed his ravaged nerves. She balanced a half-empty plate on her lap. Her honey-brown eyes blinking repeatedly spoke of her fight to stay awake. It was barely nine—six by west coast timing—but she couldn't keep her eyes open. Knowing her, she had started her day before six. And travel could be exhausting enough without suffering from a stomach ailment.

Ray strolled across the room to rescue her tilting plate. "Time for you to go to bed."

"The party is still going on," she protested as he pulled her to her feet.

"And it can continue without us." He handed her plate off to his cousin and led her to his grandmother. "Mamó, Lauren is exhausted. We're going to leave for the hotel."

"Oh, no." Mamó waved off his statement. "You're both staying here. I made up your room special for you, with new sheets and towels."

He gritted his teeth. He loved his family, but he preferred the privacy and autonomy of a hotel in the nation's largest city.

Plus, he hadn't missed the singular use of "room"—as in Lauren and him in the same sleeping quarters. He couldn't do that to Lauren. She'd already made a huge concession by allowing the faux engagement to stand. He wouldn't force her to share his room.

"We don't want to put you to extra trouble." Ray chose an explanation she'd understand. And it was true, too. "Plus I have appointments in the city."

"Oh…" Disappointment turned Mamó's smile upside down. "But we've already taken your things up to your room." Resignation rang heavy in her voice. She turned to Lauren. "Would you prefer your own room, dear? Is that it? There's a daybed in the sewing room. It's a bit dusty in there—I confess I haven't been in the room for several months—but it won't take long to spruce it up."

*Drat.* He should have had his assistant call her with his itinerary, but he'd been busy arranging siting plans with the mayor's office. Ray usually stayed in the city when he visited. He never stayed long, for precisely this reason.

He hated seeing his grandmother upset. A glance at Lauren showed her following the conversation with a slight frown drawing her delicate eyebrows together. Her sleepy eyes lifted to his and he saw the words forming on her tongue. He forestalled her so she'd know exactly what she was getting herself into.

"It's best if we go to the suite at the hotel. I did promise Lauren her own space. Plus, it's your birthday. You shouldn't have to be concerned about caring for houseguests."

"You know I don't mind. But if it's what you prefer..." All animation drained from Mamó's face. "I was so looking forward to cooking you breakfast, like old times."

Lauren reached for his hand and gave it a squeeze. "It's okay, Ray. I'm fine with staying here if you'd like."

Now he really felt torn. He'd much rather stay at the hotel, but the option of holding Lauren in his arms through the night brought a whole new element to the situation.

Generally he arranged his amorous adventures so he ended up alone in his own bed. He found it helped alleviate complications over the long haul. But for once a woman was less inclined for entanglement than he was.

In their month-long fling only one memorable encounter had occurred in a bed. He'd run into her at a hotel where she and her sister had been working a holiday party for Garrett. Ray had dragged her out a side door for a few heated moments. She'd quickly put the brakes on because she'd been working, but he'd sent a room key to her and after the event she'd met him upstairs.

It had turned out their stolen moment hadn't been as private as he'd thought, because the next morning a picture of a torrid embrace between the two of them had hit the tabloids. Who would have predicted that moment would have led to this one?

"If Lauren is okay with it, then I'm not going to say no to your pancakes."

In the end his purpose for being here motivated his decision. His worry had lifted during the party as Mamó had seemed like her old self. Watching the light fade out of her now tore at his gut. The fatigue stamped on Lauren's fine features added weight to Mamó's request. Staying here benefited both women at this point. And, truly, if he wanted to get Mamó out of her funk he needed to give a little too. Disappointing her on his first day was not a smart move.

"Excellent." Mamó clapped her hands together. "I'll show you up."

"No need." He kissed her cheek before pulling Lauren after him toward the stairs. "I know the way."

"It was a lovely party," Lauren said over her shoulder.

"Thank you, dear. I look forward to getting to know you better tomorrow."

"Goodnight, Mamó," he called.

Upstairs, he opened the door to his childhood room and ushered Lauren inside. He half expected the room to be the same as when he'd left for UCLA fifteen years ago. Luckily the movie posters, twin beds, and blue plaid bedspread were long gone. Instead the walls were painted a pale green and a queen bed stood in the middle of the room, covered by a sage comforter with brown swirls. A large rug in reverse colors was spread across the hardwood floor.

Well, most of it had changed. He grinned when he focused on the art. Movie posters, but instead of being tacked to the wall these were framed behind glass and they were posters for *his* movies.

"Nice touch." Lauren walked to the window and pulled the chocolate-brown curtains closed. "She obviously keeps up with your work."

"When I left for Los Angeles she asked me to send her memorabilia of all my work. I didn't realize it was going on the walls."

"She loves you. It was sweet of you to agree to stay."

He shrugged. It shouldn't be a big deal. It wouldn't be if his grandmother had agreed to move from this neighborhood. He felt powerless here.

"I'm not the one who wanted separate rooms," he pointed out, slowly stalking her into the corner of the room.

When her back hit the wall, her hands hit his chest.

"Stop right there." She cocked her chin up and looked down her pretty little nose at him. "Nothing has changed."

He groaned and dropped his forehead on hers. "Please don't tell me I'm going to be sleeping on the floor."

"That won't be necessary." She kissed his cheek, then slipped away. Their suitcases sat at the end of the bed and she moved to lift one of hers onto the comforter. "We'll share the bed, but the no touching rule still stands. As much as possible, anyway. We'll sleep facing away from each other."

He laughed and picked up his camera. "You're joking, right?"

"I'm not, actually." She rocked on her heels, frowning at the lens directed at her. "I don't have the energy to joke."

With her confession he realized she was actually swaying on her feet.

She pulled a toiletries bag from her case along with a nightgown. "New rule: no nudity in this room. Including socks."

"Socks?" He got the no nudity—not that he liked it. But what was the deal with socks?

"Yes, socks. No stripping down to your socks and pretending you're not naked."

He cocked his head and tugged on the end of her pale ponytail. "It sounds like you've used these rules before."

"No," she denied. "But I know how men think. So don't bother pushing the limits. Not only would it be a cop-out, but let me just warn you: the socks alone look isn't sexy."

"Don't worry—it's not a look you'll ever see on me. Now, *you*..." he leaned close to whisper in her ear "...are free to prance around in stockings anytime you want."

"Not going to happen." She used the hand clutching her nightgown to push him back. "The rules are for both of us. So do you agree?" She scowled at him until he came out from behind the camera and nodded. "Good. Now, if you don't mind, I'd like to use the bathroom first."

"Go ahead." He pointed to a door in the corner. "You can use that door or the one in the hall."

"Thank you." She skirted around him. "Quit aiming that camera at me. The rules make this a safe zone. There's no need to hide." And with that she disappeared into the bath.

He set the camera down. How did she do that? See straight to his soul?

No one had ever questioned why he carried a camera. He'd picked up Mamó's small automatic camera not long after his parents had died. Happy to have him show an interest in something—anything—she had given it to him. For a long time he had hidden behind it. It was a world he controlled. He supposed old habits died hard.

Lauren wasn't herself tonight. Sure, she'd pressed her rules on him, but she lacked her usual sass and fire. The trip had obviously taken a lot out of her. Hopefully the faint shadows under her eyes and her low energy would go away after a good night's sleep. It unsettled him to see her out of sorts. At least her stomach seemed to have settled down.

While he waited for her to finish in the bathroom he checked the dresser and found the drawers were empty. Hiking his suitcase onto the bed, he swept the contents up in one arm and dropped them into the bottom drawer.

He eyed Lauren's open case and decided to help her out. Her stuff went in the top and middle drawers. Then he emptied her garment bag into the closet. Their shoes went on top of the stacked luggage in the bottom of the closet.

Once he'd finished the unpacking he settled in the lone armchair and tapped his fingers on the brown Pleather arm. He glanced at his watch: just after ten. No way was he sleeping anytime soon. Especially in that tiny bed with Lauren tucked up next to him. Not with a no touching rule firmly in place.

*Hell.* He scrubbed his hands over his face. It was bad enough being back in his old neighborhood, with all the memories waiting to trip him up, now he had to deal with a faux engagement.

He closed his eyes and just for a moment pretended it was real, that he and Lauren were on the brink of starting a life together. He saw the future spread out before him, complete with Lauren at his side and a beaming Mamó cradling a baby in her arms. The wonder of it felt so real he had to shut it down.

The shower was turned off in the next room. He walked over and gave a brief knock. A muffled acknowledgement came from the other side.

"Hey, I'm going to rejoin the party for a while."

The door opened a crack and one golden eye peeked at him. "Okay, thanks for letting me know."

"Leave space for me," he taunted her, hoping to spark some of her fire.

"I will," was her quiet response. "Goodnight."

"Night." He sighed.

The door closed. He pressed his hand to the wood and assured himself she'd be her old self in the morning. Then he grabbed his camera off the dresser and headed back to the party, the option of spending time with the matriarchs of his old neighborhood only slightly better than the torture of lying awake in a platonic bed with Lauren.

Lauren leaned against the bathroom door until she heard the bedroom door click. The door of the bedroom she shared with Ray Donovan.

What had she been thinking?

She'd been so careful to outline her conditions for accompanying Ray, with separate rooms right at the top. Plain and simple: Mamó had got to her. The pleading in her eyes, the resignation on her face... Until that moment Lauren hadn't seen the depression Ray feared, but seeing the loneliness in the older woman's eyes had made Lauren sad. No way could she deny her. Lauren loved her family, and couldn't imagine her mother's reaction if she tried to stay at a hotel when she visited.

Of course not every family was as close as hers. How she longed for a cuddle with her mom.

Wanting to take advantage of Ray's absence, she hurried to brush her teeth and slip into her nightshirt—an oversized T-shirt that fell to her knees and hung off her shoulder. It was the most comfortable and least appealing sleep garment in her wardrobe. She'd brought it for the comfort, but was glad for its lack of allure now she was sharing with Ray.

Yawning, she moved into the bedroom. The thought of unpacking filled her with dread. Her limbs felt so heavy she could barely lift them. The bed looked inviting. She wanted nothing more than to pull back the comforter and climb in.

*Wait.* She blinked at the empty spread. Where did her suitcase go?

She scuffed around to the other side, thinking Ray must have set it aside. *Nope.* Next she opened the top drawer of the dresser. She stared down at the contents, blinked, and stared a moment more, her mind slow to accept the notion of Ray unpacking for her. But there was the evidence.

Tears stung her eyes. How sweet. Seriously, she could kiss the man.

Good thing he wasn't around or she might break another rule.

The contents of the drawer needed straightening, but it was good enough for tonight. She tucked her dirty clothes into a corner and shoved the drawer closed. All things considered, Ray had been pretty decent today—taking care of her, sticking to the rules even when it upset his grandmother, unpacking her things.

Well, except for the kiss on the plane.

She pressed her lips together to squash the smile tugging at the corner of her mouth. She would *not* let the man seduce her again. No doubt he'd be back to his regular dictatorial self tomorrow. She'd be better able to deal with him then.

Giving in to her weariness, she burrowed into the queen bed, staying strictly to her side.

After all, rules were rules.

Mamó fell asleep in her chair as the last guests were leaving. Ray helped Kyla and Ellie on cleanup by carrying the dirty dishes to the kitchen while they put the food away and loaded the dishwasher. When he came back from taking out the trash, Aunt Ellie shooed Kyla off to bed.

Kyla folded her dishtowel and hung it over the stove handle. "Only because I have work in the morning." She stopped by Ray to kiss his cheek. "Welcome home."

He punched her in the arm. "Good to see you, too."

"Ow! That hurt." Rubbing her arm, she made for the door leading next door. "Bully."

"Girl."

"And proud of it. Night, Mom." Kyla stuck her tongue out at Ray just before she disappeared.

He grinned and turned to his aunt, slipping his arm around her shoulder. "It's good to be home." He nodded toward Mamó. "How is she doing?"

"Sound as an old horse. But she's been down a lot lately. It was good to see her so up tonight. You being here is going to be good for her."

"I hope so." His gut clutched at the concern in his aunt's eyes. "Don't they have meds for depression these days?"

"Yes, but she wouldn't take them even if she agreed to go to the doctor and get properly diagnosed. You know how she is about taking medicine. I've been checking out the internet to find natural remedies through diet and exercise."

"That sounds great."

"Of course the best thing would be—"

"For me to get married? Come on, Ellie, that's not fair.

And announcing it to the neighbors isn't going to magically make it happen."

Ellie groaned. "I know. I'm so sorry."

"Oh, I know where to place the blame. And we'll be talking in the morning."

"Don't be too hard on her. Mrs. Renwicki was being particularly obnoxious about Camilla—going on about her expecting her third child. Not only was Mom upset on your behalf, but I'm sure she was thinking those could have been *her* great-grandkids."

"Not in this lifetime."

"No, of course not. Obviously Mom lost it for a moment there."

All too familiar with Mamó's desire for him to marry and produce a great-grandbaby, Ray rolled his head over the hunched muscles of his shoulders. To keep from giving her false hope was one of the reasons he kept his affairs private.

"Yeah, well, it's not just me she's involved in her fabrication," he reminded his aunt.

"Gosh, you're right." Ellie's worried gaze went to the ceiling, towards where his room was situated. "Will Lauren try to take advantage?"

He barked out a laugh. "Not likely. But there were a lot of people who bore witness to Mamó's announcement."

"Oh." Ellie covered her mouth with her fingers. "You think someone will leak the news? But these are friends of the family."

"Who will see nothing wrong with sharing the knowledge with their friends and family. So, yeah, I expect word to get to the press within a couple of days."

Something he needed to warn Lauren about. She might not have been so quick to give in to Mamó if she'd realized the news would become public.

Which meant he owed her an apology as well as his appreciation.

"Ray…" Ellie fretted, regret in her hazel eyes.

"Don't worry about it. I'll call my assistant, get him started on damage control." He gave her a kiss on the cheek. "Do you need help getting her to bed?"

"No." She patted his hand. "I've got her. I just need to finish cleaning up. You head on up. I hope we weren't too overwhelming for Lauren?"

"No, she'll be fine. She's close with her family so she gets it."

"Good. She seems nice."

"She is." *To most people.* She liked to bust his chops, but he knew she'd get along with his family. If only to spite him. He actually looked forward to her giving him guff again. It would mean she was back to her old self.

"Why don't you take care of Mamó and I'll finish up here?"

"I can't let you do that."

"Sure you can. I'm on California time. I need to kill an hour before I'll be ready to sleep."

Begrudgingly she nodded. "It's good to have you home."

She shook Mamó awake and led his sleepy grandmother down the hall toward her bedroom.

Pulling open the dishwasher, he started loading in more dishes. Memories flooded in. Back in the day he and Mamó had had the routine down to a science and had been able to finish up in ten minutes or less.

He loved her. But she'd put him in quite a fix. He suspected that Lauren would be cool about the whole engagement thing, but in reality she could end up suing him for breach of promise when he failed to marry her. She knew he'd pay. Because no way would he humiliate Mamó by letting the whole thing play out in the news.

It had been a long time since he'd been able to trust a woman.

Fifteen years, to be exact—ever since Camilla had taught him that you never truly knew anyone. He couldn't bring himself to be happy for her. Not after what she'd cost him. So he was petty? He'd live with it.

Dishes loaded, he poured in dishwashing crystals, closed and locked the door, and set the machine in motion. Lauren thought of him as controlling and manipulative. He'd live with that, too. And place the blame right at Camilla's feet.

After drying his hands on the dishtowel, he wiped down the counter.

He'd never be caught unprepared again.

# CHAPTER FIVE

LAUREN AWOKE SLOWLY. Her first thought was for the state of her stomach. When there was no immediate revolt her senses began to pick up on other elements. Like the large, muscular man she was snuggled up to.

Her eyes flew open to the yummy sight of smooth skin covering broad shoulders. She reared back, ready to scold Ray for taking advantage, only to find she'd been the one to encroach on *his* side of the bed.

Chagrined at being the one to break the rules, she rolled back to her side and immediately missed his warmth. Obviously she'd been lured by his heat during the night until she'd wrapped herself around him. With any luck he'd slept through her lapse, otherwise he'd razz her unmercifully for breaking her own rules.

She waited for him to move, to awake. When a few minutes passed and he didn't shift, she slid from the bed and fled to the bathroom. Several minutes later she stood brushing her teeth when the door from the bedroom opened and Ray strolled in.

"Morning." He gave her a peck on the cheek, then moved past her to the shower. Dropping his gray knit boxers, he stepped naked into the tub and pulled the curtain closed. Lauren choked on a mouthful of toothpaste.

She spit, rinsed, grabbed her make-up bag and escaped to the bedroom to dress before he finished showering. It didn't take long to pull on jeans and a lavender sweater. She tugged on thick socks and low-heeled boots, and then sat on the side of the bed to put her make-up on, consciously waiting for Ray to make his appearance.

Her stomach hadn't protested yet, but she snagged a soda cracker from her purse stash. Better safe than sorry. Yesterday's queasiness had been explained away with the travel, but it couldn't continue without serious questions arising.

Lauren preferred to tell Ray about his impending fatherhood on her own terms, at her own pace. Which might well be when they were back in California—not while she was half a world away from her support system. Or trying to keep up the pretense of a false engagement.

He wandered into the bedroom, a towel hitched around lean hips.

"Seriously?" she demanded. "You agreed to the rules!"

His bare shoulders were impossibly wide and the muscles in his arms and chest flexed as he rubbed a second towel over his head. The man was droolworthy, with his sculpted abs, tight gluteus, and long, hair-dusted legs. Just watching him walk across the room made her mouth water. Other body parts went straight to tingle.

This was exactly why she'd made the rules.

He glanced over his shoulder at her. "I've honored them." He stepped into a pair of boxer briefs before ditching the towel. "We never discussed the bathroom. Plus, let me just repeat how crazy I think they are. It's not like we haven't—"

"I know we've been intimate." Didn't matter. They'd never been naked together. Their encounters had been too hurried, too frantic. "But that's over."

"So you say." He grabbed a pair of chinos from the bottom drawer, along with a pale blue T-shirt. "I thought you might have changed your mind."

Her hands went to her hips. "What made you think that?"

"The way you cozied up to me in bed last night, for one."

Heat flooded her cheeks. So much for the hope he'd slept through her groping. "That was unintentional," she informed him. "It won't happen again."

"If it was unintentional…" he came to tower over her "…that means you had no control over your actions. What makes you so sure it won't happen again?"

She lifted her chin. "I was overly tired last night. That won't be a problem the rest of the trip."

"I hope you're right." He lifted his right hand, cupped her cheek, and traced the faint shadows under her eye. "Not that I'm complaining. I won't hold you to the rules. Feel free to cozy up to me anytime you please."

"I'm not going to hold you to a standard I'm not willing to uphold myself." She backed up until his hand dropped. "The rules are meant as a mutual show of respect. Is it too much to ask for your cooperation?"

"Not at all—but then I'm not the one trying to pretend our relationship never happened."

Her jaw dropped. "Oh, believe me, I'm well aware that our…fling…*happened*." Knowledge of their child ran deep within her. "And calling what was between us a relationship is pushing it, don't you think?"

"I don't generally say things I don't mean." He cocked his head, invading her space again. "Hurried and hot doesn't necessarily relate to lack of depth."

"Funny, that's exactly how I see it." She locked her knees, refusing to give him any more ground.

"Is that what bothers you?" he asked, all concern, and she was reminded again that he had started his career as an actor. "You doubt my commitment?"

"I have no doubt of your commitment…" she paused "…to getting your own way." She circled him and crossed the room. "Look, I admit the sex was hot. It was crazy and wild and fun. But it was totally lacking in emotional depth.

And that's not who I am." Hand on the doorknob, she met his gaze. "I smell coffee. We should go down."

Ray followed Lauren down the stairs, enjoying the sway of her hips in the well-fitting jeans. She had him in a quandary. She'd nailed his motivation dead-on, but she was also wrong.

His emotions were not as detached as she believed. He'd be a whole lot more comfortable if they were.

Instead he worried about the pallor in her cheeks and whether she had slept well the night before. Now he had her back in his life he wanted to explore the passion between them at a more leisurely pace.

When he'd finally joined her in the tiny bed he'd lain awake for a good hour, tormented by his promise not to touch. He'd stared into the dark while she'd shifted from position to position, as if unable to get comfortable. She'd seemed drawn to him, yet had jerked away if she got too close. Her subconscious was clearly on the job.

Her restlessness had added to his until he'd finally had enough. He'd rolled over and gathered her in his arms, tucking her into the shelter of his body. She'd sighed and gone limp in his arms. Despite the arousal intensified by her nearness, he'd soon followed her into sleep.

Thankfully she blamed their tangled bodies on their subconscious actions. Yeah, that was a confession he'd take to his grave.

In the kitchen Mamó stood at the stove, flipping pancakes. When she heard them on the stairs she turned with a huge smile.

"Good morning." She greeted Lauren and then Ray. "Sit. Sit. As promised, I have your favorite breakfast." She bustled to the stove and returned with a heaping platter she set in the middle of the table. "Blueberry pancakes."

"Mamó, this looks wonderful." Lauren helped herself to one pancake.

"They *are* wonderful." Ray added another to her plate. "Nobody can eat just one," he explained piling four onto his plate. He added warm syrup and dug in.

"He's right, dear." Mamó poured him a cup of coffee, then held the pot over Lauren's cup.

Lauren stopped her. "Do you have decaffeinated?"

Mamó grimaced. "Unfortunately, I do. But it's instant."

"That'll work." Lauren hopped up. "I'll get it. You sit with Ray. I'm sure you have a lot of catching up to do." Before his grandmother could protest, Lauren added, "That is if you don't mind if I make myself at home?"

"Of course, my dear." Mamó slid into the chair next to Ray as she directed Lauren to the proper cabinet. "I want you to be comfortable."

Ray silently toasted Lauren for the brilliant move. She met his salute with a smile and started the microwave. He turned his attention to Mamó.

"Great party last night. Thanks for the welcome."

"Everyone was so excited to see you." Mamó patted his hand. "It's been too long since you visited the neighborhood. They're so happy for your success."

"And apparently for my engagement." He eyed her over his coffee mug.

Mamó's chin lowered and her shoulders sagged. "I'm sorry," she apologized. Then she spoiled it by claiming, "It's your own fault—staying away so long, never giving me any news to share."

"The fact I haven't been back to the neighborhood for a while is not an excuse for lying to your friends."

She stared down at the table, twisted her mug between sturdy hands marked by age and wear. "I wouldn't have to lie if you'd make more of an effort."

He ignored that. Attacking her was not the way to bolster her up. But he couldn't let her get away with this behavior either.

"It's one thing if it were just me." He let the words hang

in the air for a moment. "But you've put Lauren in a difficult position."

A frown pulled Mamó's hand-drawn brows together. "Oh, but —"

Ray cut Lauren's protest off with a flick of his eyes and a shake of his head. "It's not okay, Lauren. When we start getting pestered by the press you won't feel so generous."

"Press?" She bit her pretty bottom lip.

"If it hasn't hit the social media outlets yet, it will soon." He hardened his heart. Soft-pedaling the news wouldn't help anyone. "Phone calls requesting confirmation won't be far behind."

She pushed away from the table. "Excuse me."

"Where are you going?" he asked.

"To text my family and warn them that rumors of my engagement are grossly exaggerated."

"You can do that from here." He looked at her plate, pleased to see she'd eaten both pancakes.

"I could, but my mom will be calling two seconds after she gets the message, so I'll take it to the next room. I'd be dealing with Tori, too, except she's halfway around the world on her honeymoon. No telling when she'll call."

"It's pretty early in California," Ray reminded her.

Lauren glanced at the kitchen clock. "Not early enough."

She took off, and Ray arched a brow at Mamó.

"It was just a few friends." Mamó avoided his gaze. Instead she fussed with the syrup pitcher, wiping the edge and replacing it in the middle of the table.

"Friends gossip," he reminded her.

"Doris Renwicki was the troublemaker." Mamó lifted contrite eyes to meet his gaze. "I really am sorry. She just got to me, with all her talk of babies."

"I know." He covered her hand with his. The woman had gotten to him, too. So, yeah, he understood. But that didn't mean he could let Mamó off the hook. His career was too public to have odd announcements like this popping up. Luckily he was here and could coordinate damage control.

"You've put Lauren and me in a difficult situation. If I were serious and had decided to ask her to marry me, you've stolen her moment of announcing it. And that's if she doesn't question my motives and agrees to accept my proposal."

"Oh, Ray, of course she'd accept you." Mamó covered her mouth, true distress in her pale eyes. "But you're right. I've ruined her moment. Do you think she can forgive me?"

Figured she would zero in on the injury to Lauren.

"What can I do?" She began to cry. "I don't want things to be difficult between the two of you."

*Damn.* This wasn't what he wanted. He pushed his empty plate to the side.

"Stop crying. Don't worry. I'll fix it."

"I'm sorry." She wiped at her eyes.

"I know, and I'm going to fix it. Just stop crying now. Lauren will think I'm being mean."

"It's not you, it's me." She hid her face in a napkin.

"It'll be okay." Her distress made his gut clench. He took her hand in his and squeezed.

"It won't. The press will come."

"I'll handle it," he promised, going around the table to pull her into his arms. "I love you, Mamó. Now, dry your eyes. You want to be beautiful for your party."

"I don't want to go."

"Of course you do. It's just the thing to cheer you up. Everything is going to be okay."

"No. I've messed things up for you and Lauren."

"When I'm done fixing things she'll think I'm a hero."

Mamó's body stopped shaking. "A hero, huh?"

A warm jacket was settled over Lauren's shoulders and she turned to give Ray a grateful smile. As expected, her mom had called right on the heels of Lauren's text. Wanting privacy for the call, she'd stepped outside onto Mamó's tiny stoop, only to discover it had snowed overnight. The overhang protected the stoop and some of the steps, so she wasn't standing in snow, but her sweater did little to ward off the freezing temperature.

"Don't worry. You'll be the first to know," she reassured her mother for the third time. "Ray's waiting for me. I have to go."

"Okay, but I want the whole story when you get home," warned her mom. "Say hello to Ray for me. Bye, love you."

"Love you." Lauren closed her phone. "Thanks for the jacket," she said to Ray. "It snowed."

"It does that here."

"Tori would be so jealous."

Making it snow at his Hollywood manor had been Garrett's Christmas gift to her twin. The romantic gesture had won Tori's heart and the acceptance of his proposal. Lauren still got choked up thinking about it. Here in New York she found the reality of the frozen landscape a bit overwhelming.

"So, did you haul Mamó over the coals?"

He cocked his head. "It felt like it. She cried."

"I'm sorry." She slipped her arms into his jacket. "But you needed to talk to her. It would be bad enough if you were an average guy. Right now you're the hottest director in the country. The press will be all over this. Is she okay?"

"Yeah." He flicked at a piece of paper. "I distracted her by asking after her 'to-do' list. Are you up for doing some chores?"

"Sure I'll help," she agreed easily. "I'm not about to pass up the opportunity to watch the great Ray Donovan at manual labor."

Just the notion had her insides tingling.

"Brat." He tugged on her ponytail. "Such wit. You should consider writing for the movies."

"Oh, no." Even though he'd joked, she literally backed

away at his suggestion. "That's your world, not mine. I'm happy staying in the background, thank you very much."

"You're good with details." He edged forward, eliminating the distance she'd created between them.

He always did that, and had done right from the beginning of their association. Even before they'd become intimate. It was intoxicating and unnerving at the same time.

"You'd make an excellent production assistant."

"I have a job, but thanks for the endorsement."

She inched back again, seeking the space she needed. Seriously, how was she supposed to keep a clear head around him while constantly inhaling the clean, male scent of him?

"What's on the to-do list?"

He consulted the paper. "A broken railing, changing some lightbulbs, and assembling a console."

"That's quite a list. We should get started if we want to finish before the party." Shivering, she tucked her hands in the pockets of his jacket. "Are there home improvement centers in New York?"

"Better. We have Chester's Hardware."

He invaded her bubble again, but a car pulling to a stop in front of the house distracted her. Had the press discovered them already?

A uniformed deliveryman emerged from the car, carrying a large box. He crunched through the snow, opened the gate, and approached the steps. "Delivery for Lauren Randall."

Her brows zinged up in surprise. She wasn't expecting anything—certainly not at this address.

"I'm Lauren Randall." She accepted the package, thinking she should tip the man. She glanced up at Ray. "My purse is inside."

"That's okay, ma'am," the delivery person assured her. "The tip was included. Have a nice day, now." He tipped his head and trudged back to his car.

She clutched the large package to her. "For a minute there I thought the press had found us."

"Actually, I see a fellow across the way with a camera." A hand in the small of her back urged her toward the door. "Why don't we take this inside?"

Her skin itched at the idea of being spied on, so she allowed him to direct her indoors.

She settled on the sofa and placed the large box next to her. "What did you do, Ray?"

"What makes you think it's from me?" He went to the fire and tossed on a log, then took up a spot at the mantel.

"Because nobody knows I'm here."

"Open it."

Eying him suspiciously, she worked off the bright red bow. Was it coincidence that the bow was her favorite color or had Ray asked for red? Coincidence, surely? She doubted Ray knew her favorite color.

She lifted off the lid and dug through mounds of tissue. Her heart began an erratic tattoo as she recognized the famous name blazoned on the inside of the box. Maybe he did know, because the paper parted to reveal a red leather coat trimmed in black fur. *Oh, my.*

"Oh, my..." Mamó echoed Lauren's thoughts. "What a beautiful coat."

Lauren held the garment up. The jacket was long enough to hit her just above the knee. A black asymmetrical zipper slashed across the front and the softest of faux fur lined the inside from shoulder to hem, including a shawl collar that converted into a hood.

"Gorgeous..." she breathed.

"Try it on," Mamó urged.

Lauren didn't need the encouragement. She had already unzipped the jacket and shrugged out of Ray's coat. She slid her arms in and sighed as softness and warmth surrounded her. The smell of rich leather teased her nostrils. Oh, she coveted it.

She turned to Ray, who smirked with quiet satisfaction.

"Thank you," she said as she shrugged out of the lovely coat. "But I can't accept it."

"Oh, but—" Mamó covered her mouth, turned around, and hurried toward the kitchen.

Ellie came through the connecting door to her unit and Mamó detoured to grab her arm and drag her along to the back of the house.

Lauren barely noticed. All her attention was focused on Ray's stormy expression.

"You need a warmer jacket. Your time on the stoop should have proved that."

"I'll manage."

For some reason her refusal seemed to hurt him. But accepting such an expensive gift implied an intimacy she was trying to avoid. She'd told him she didn't need a new coat, and yet true to his controlling nature he'd gone against her wishes and bought one anyway.

"It's too much."

"I can afford it."

"That's not the point."

"You just said it was." He raked a hand through his hair. "You're only here because of me. It's my responsibility to make sure you don't suffer for doing me a favor."

Silently she applauded him for the brilliant argument, but she saw right through him and chided him with a simple, "Ray…"

"As far as I'm concerned it's yours," he said dismissively. "If you don't want it, just borrow it while you're here and I'll have Mamó give it to the Salvation Army when we leave. Whatever you decide, I'm leaving for the hardware store in ten minutes."

He stormed off, taking the stairs two at a time.

Dang the man. By stating his intention to give the coat away to charity he'd taken the power of her refusal away from her. She stroked the silky black faux fur. Would it hurt to wear it during her visit?

*Yes.* She needed to stand by her principles—to show him she couldn't be bullied or bought. Regretfully, she folded the jacket back into the box. Sometimes being right really, *really* sucked.

# CHAPTER SIX

OF COURSE THEY walked to Chester's. The neighborhood store turned out to be only three blocks away. It was easier to go by foot than to shovel the drifts away from the garage. Ray offered to call a cab, but Lauren refused. Not for three blocks.

She slid into her fleece-lined raincoat, borrowed Ellie's snow boots, and met Ray at the gate.

He scowled at her coat but refrained from saying anything. Instead he took her arm. "Be careful. The snow has been shoveled, but it can be slick."

At first they strolled in silence, but several people were out and Ray got hailed a number of times. He tried to keep them moving, which proved difficult when it was someone on the same side of the street.

Shivering as a light snow began to fall, Lauren admired his skillful ability to greet and go. Across the way she noticed the photographer Ray had spotted earlier. The man kept pace with them, yet seemed content to keep his distance.

All in all, by the time they reached the hardware store, she wished she hadn't been quite so quick to set Ray's gift aside.

"Here we are." He held the door for her.

Grateful for the promise of warmth, she stepped inside. She stamped the snow from her boots and faced Ray. Only to find he'd all but disappeared. A knit cap covered his hair, his neck scarf had been pulled up to cover the bottom half of his face, and his shoulders were slumped forward. He'd gone from being a confident, dynamic man who dominated any room he entered to a man most people would overlook. Obviously that was the point.

Considering their trip here, she couldn't blame him. On this Tuesday morning Chester's hopped with clientele.

"Hello, I'm Lauren." She offered Ray her gloved hand. "Who are *you*?"

"Ha-ha." He took her hand and gave her a basket to carry before leading her deeper into the store. "You're a real comedian."

"Sorry, I couldn't resist. It's a very effective disguise. Do you have to use it often?"

"No." He turned down an aisle and stopped in front of an assortment of lubricating oils. He handed her a can and took off again. "I'm not in front of the cameras anymore, so I'm not as recognizable as celebrities on TV or in movies. Then there's the fact most people are too intimidated to approach me. But this is my old neighborhood, so all bets are off."

"Everyone seems happy for your success. And you're very gracious with them. Yet you're also careful to keep them at a distance." She followed him into the lighting aisle. "Kyla said it's been years since you've visited Mamó at home."

"Do you have a point?" His gaze roamed the shelves, seeking three-way bulbs.

"I'm just wondering what you're running from?"

He went totally still.

Giving him time, she reached past him and selected energy-saving three-way bulbs. She placed them in the basket and waited for him to come back to her. His reaction confirmed her suspicion.

Ray hadn't willingly abandoned his neighborhood. Something had sent him running.

Finally he shrugged. "We all have things in our past we'd rather forget."

"True." She hooked her arm through his. "But some stick with us more than others."

"Will you wear the coat?"

She rolled her eyes. Leave it to him to manipulate his own confession. Too bad she had him beat. "Oh, yeah. I already made that decision on the walk over here. I may be stubborn. I'm not stupid."

"Right." He grinned and reclaimed the basket. He held his other hand out to her. "Come on. Time to go play handyman."

"No touching," she said, reminding herself as well as him, and walked around him to the cashier.

Back at the house, Lauren gratefully released her end of the heavy box containing the mahogany console. They'd blown through the fix-it items on Mamó's to-do list and were about to put together the new console table.

Lauren read the directions while he went straight to sorting the nails and screws. When she caught herself staring at his bent head, she decided to press him a little more on his past.

She crouched down next to him. "So, about those things in the past you prefer to forget…sometimes it helps to share."

"I appreciate the offer." He stroked his thumb over the dent in her chin. "It's better left buried."

"I disagree." She blew out a breath. "I don't know if Garrett told you this, but Tori and I had a friend in high school who committed suicide."

"He mentioned it." His shuttered gaze met hers before he focused on lining up the planks by size.

She stood and squared her shoulders. This was never easy to talk about.

"Well, the school provided counseling for those that

wanted it, and because we were particularly close to him my parents continued it for an extra month. There was guilt and anger to deal with, as well as loss and sorrow. Mostly for Tori. I went more to support her. By talking about our experience we were able to gain perspective and work our way through the stages of grief in a healthy manner."

He slowly rose to his feet to stare down into her eyes. "And yet Tori's memories of that time almost cost her her relationship with Garrett."

"Talking about it doesn't take away the importance of an event. But it can minimize its power over you. Once you've shared with someone, the worst that can happen is over. Someone else knows. The fear of discovery is past, making it easier to deal with what follows."

"Really? Because having the whole neighborhood witness my humiliation, pain and disappointment didn't make it easier to bear. I call *liar* on that."

She flinched—more at what he had revealed than at the bite in his words.

"I once let a man control me to the point I almost ditched my family for him." Saying it out loud sent a cold wave down her spine. Her throat clenched. It was her biggest shame. And she had no idea why she'd just told him. Who knew being pregnant led to insanity? Worse, she couldn't seem to stop. "It was a form of abuse that I didn't even see happening."

"Oh, Lauren." He pulled her into his arms. The screwdriver in his hand bumped against her butt. He set it aside, then enfolded her in a tender embrace. "I just can't see it. You're so in control, so strong."

"In a way, that just made it worse. It was subtle and insidious and completely undermined who I was. Tori saved me."

And for a while Lauren had hated her for it.

"When I finally made the break from Brad I couldn't talk to Mom or Tori. I was too ashamed. That fear of discovery... But I remembered the counseling from high school and decided to see if my college provided counselors and I was able to talk to someone."

She'd learned only she had the ability to give her power away.

His hand stroked softly through her hair. Allowing him to hold her like this broke the rules, but she couldn't bring herself to care. Insanity aside, she'd started this in order to help him deal with whatever it was that had driven him away from Queens.

She eased away. "I can promise you nothing is as bad as you build it up to be in your own head."

He cupped the back of her neck, his intent gaze scrutinizing her carefully. "You're such a contradiction. You find it hard to accept a gift but now you've bared your soul for me."

A shrug was all she had to give him. "Different cost values."

He rocked his forehead over hers. "I don't know what to say."

"The point is your secrets are safe with me. You can say anything." She pressed her lips to his cheek before stepping back again. "And I have agreed to wear the jacket, so technically you owe me."

"I'll think about it."

"A little more your way," Ray directed, eyeing the entryway to gauge its center point. "Okay, set it down."

Lauren stepped back to view the finished results as Ray added baskets to the bottom shelf of the console. Thirty inches high and five feet long, it had three deep drawers across the front, with three rattan baskets going in the open slots below the drawers.

"It really is a lovely piece." She held her hand up for a high-five. "Well done, Donovan."

He slapped her palm. "I couldn't have done it without you, Randall."

"Seriously," she agreed, "that was one heavy beast."

He yanked on the end of her ponytail. "We make a good team."

"Hmm..."

She hummed the noncommittal response just to be contrary. Surprisingly, they had worked well together, making fairly quick work of the assembly. Still, after getting all touchy-feely with him it was best not to give him too much encouragement. The man didn't know the meaning of boundaries. Give him an inch and he'd take a mile.

Best not to encourage herself either.

More than once she'd caught herself staring at his hands. Remembering how they felt on her skin. Long-fingered, strong, and competent, his broad-palmed hands were sensual tools of torment, capable of sending her senses reeling.

Oh, yeah, he knew how to use his hands.

"Mamó will be thrilled." She forced her attention back to the moment.

"I think so." He glanced at his watch. "They should be back soon."

Ellie had whisked Mamó off to the hair salon after lunch. Her big birthday bash at the community center started at six and the women were off beautifying themselves for the event.

"Hair and nails for both of them?" She shook her head while stifling a yawn. Every time she slowed down sleep tugged at her eyelids. Must be jet lag. "It'll probably be another hour at least." She bent and stuffed plastic bags into a large cardboard box. "Why don't you grab us a couple of sodas and I'll finish cleaning up here?"

"I have a better idea." He took the box from her. "Why don't you sit down while I take care of this and get the sodas? It's the least I can do after all your help."

"I won't say no."

He headed outside with the box.

She checked her phone for messages, smiled at the

text from her assistant confirming all was set for the party tonight.

Curling into the corner of the sofa, she clicked on the TV. A reality show came on in which brides sought the perfect dress. A secret fan, she rested her head on a closed fist and watched as the bride and her mother clashed over a peek-a-boo corset dress.

She fought off a yawn. Earlier she'd stepped outside to make a few arrangements for tonight's big bash. Events were Lauren's "thing." She felt bad, sitting back and doing nothing for Mamó's party, so she'd reached out to a couple of local connections she'd met at national conferences and arranged for a little something extra.

Which reminded her—she needed to fill Ray in on her plan. Her eyes closed. She struggled to push them open. Hopefully Ray wouldn't object to her interference. It was all meant in good fun…

After disposing of the box and grabbing two cans of soda from the refrigerator, Ray joined Lauren on the sofa. The first thing he noticed was that Lauren was sound asleep. Jet lag, no doubt. Compelled by something bigger than his promises, he gave in to the urge to touch. He swept a silky blond tendril behind her ear, traced the oval curve of her jaw, stroked his thumb over the plump bow of her lips.

So strong, yet so delicate. His gut churned at the thought of her under another man's thumb. Never would he have suspected her of subjugating her will to someone else. Not with the grief she gave him.

An abusive experience sure explained her fierce need for independence.

His fingers curled into a fist as he fought the desire to smash something—preferably the abusive jerk's face. Too bad he was beyond Ray's reach. Slowly he unfurled each finger, because Lauren deserved tenderness and understanding. He wouldn't be responsible for bringing her any more pain.

Dropping his hand to her thigh, he turned his attention to the TV. His brows plummeted into a scowl. What kind of hot mess had she been watching? A woman in a robe was extolling the virtues of some man while a salesclerk waded through a forest of white gowns. Some sort of bride show.

*Just kill him now.*

He picked up the remote, ready to click it away. The picture changed to a young, dark-haired woman with brown eyes in a round face. His finger froze on the remote. For a moment he saw Camilla standing there. In a blink the resemblance disappeared.

He scrubbed at the back of his neck. He obviously had the past on his mind.

Hard not to when he was smack in the middle of the borough where it had all gone down. All he wanted was to put the past behind him. Yet everywhere he looked he stumbled across reminders of his darkest moment. And Lauren's probing didn't help.

Maybe he should talk to her. *No.* He appreciated her sharing her past with him, but he couldn't reciprocate. Exposing his shame would be like opening a vein. Better to leave it buried.

Aiming the remote again, he changed the channel, finding a hockey game to watch. He settled into the cushions, one hand on Lauren's thigh, the other wrapped around a cold soda. Now, *this* was more like it. An hour alone to enjoy a cold drink, a good game, and his girl. This was the way to relax.

"Here we are, ladies." Ray climbed out of the taxi and held the door for Mamó and Lauren. He escorted them inside, where the three of them checked their coats. Ellie and Kyla had gone on ahead of them. "May I say it's my pleasure to be accompanying the two most beautiful women at the party?"

"Thank you." Pleased with his compliment, Mamó twittered while patting her white-gray crown of curls. She glowed in a jacket dress of bright purple. A dusting of soft rose highlighted the natural color in her creamy cheeks. She looked lovely, and clearly ready to party.

He wrapped her in a gentle hug. "Make sure you behave yourself."

"Where's the fun in that?" She patted his cheek, giving him a wicked smile. "I plan to party hearty tonight."

"Mamó!"

"Leave her alone." Lauren hooked her arm through his. "This is *her* night. Let her enjoy it."

"Thank you, dear." With a flash of her diamond eternity ring, Mamó waved and walked into the hall.

"'Party hearty'?" Ray muttered. "She's seventy-six."

"She's still a vibrant woman with a huge capacity for love. I know of at least one gentleman attracted by her *joie de vivre*."

Lauren dragged her hand down his arm, over his hand, clung to his fingertips for just a second, then swung around and through the door behind his grandmother.

He was distracted by her touch, by the sheer grace of her in a sassy off-the-shoulder black dress, and her words didn't connect at first. He hadn't been paying lip service when he'd told them he was with the two most beautiful women at the party. Where Mamó was lovely, Lauren literally stole his breath. *Stunning* was the only word to do her justice.

The black dress clung to soft curves, its hem flirting with the silky skin three inches above her knees. The dark color contrasted sharply with her creamy complexion, giving the impression of delicate strength. Light shimmered in her blond hair, flowing like molten gold around her shoulders as she glanced back at him. A daring red lip gloss drew his gaze to her lush mouth.

He followed as if beckoned.

Only when she disappeared from sight did her words slam into him.

Wait—a "gentleman" was interested in Mamó? Not if *he* had anything to say about it.

He rushed through the door. And found Mamó and Lauren surrounded by a bevy of young studs dressed in tuxedos. Heavens, it was like a casting call for a Fred Astaire remake.

*Oh, hell, no.*

He waded through the throng to Lauren's side and heard the last of the introductions.

"And I'm Chad," a tall man said.

He had a square chin, brown eyes and dark hair. Ray eyed the other four. Not so young after all—which only made it worse.

"I hope you will save the first dance for me?"

"Oh, my." Mamó giggled as the man lifted her hand to his mouth. "I think I can do that."

*Giggled.* Like a girl. His seventy-six-year-old grandmother.

"What's going on here?" he demanded, making no effort to curb the edge in his voice.

"Oh. Everyone—this is my grandson Ray." Mamó beamed as she made the introductions. "Ray, these lovely gentlemen are here to dance with me."

"I beg your pardon."

"Now, don't be a grouch. Lauren arranged it. I love to dance, and with so many more ladies than men this ensures I'll always have a partner." She took the opportunity to give Lauren a huge hug. "Thank you so much. It's going to be the best party ever."

"You're welcome." Lauren kissed her cheek. "I might have to borrow one myself if Ray's going to be a partypoop."

"I won't blame you." Mamó stepped back and smoothed her hands over her hips. "I should find Ellie."

"May I escort you to the head table?" Chad offered his arm.

"You may." Mamó threaded her arm through his with another giggle. The two moved off and the other men melted away.

Ray crossed his arms over his chest, his gaze narrowed on Lauren. "*You* did this?"

"This?"

"Arranged for my grandmother to be groped by a gigolo."

Her tinkling laugh grated over his taut nerves.

"They are *not* gigolos. They're dancers. I noticed a lot of Mamó's friends were single, so I called a friend of mine who arranged for a local dance studio to send over some men to act as stag dance partners."

Okay, it was a nice gesture. He still didn't like it.

"I didn't know you knew anybody in New York."

"I have contacts all over the world. We meet at conferences and trade shows. Events is a pretty small community, actually."

"I imagine you're a league above most of your colleagues."

She lifted one shoulder in a half-shrug. "No, we just have a more elite clientele than most."

"I've seen your work. I would argue you attract an elite clientele because of your above-par work." He looked around the room at the lush floral centerpieces and the billowing folds of white silk draped from the ceiling and cascading down the walls. "I can see your touch in more than the expanded guest list."

"Mamó has graciously opened her home to me. She, Ellie and Kyla have made me feel welcome. It was the least I could do."

He studied her for a long minute. She was wrong. She was a guest. Nothing had been expected of her. Not even a gift, as they were optional. In fact, in a very real way *she* was a gift—from him to his grandmother.

"I'm not sure I approve." He pulled her close and pressed a light kiss to her lips. "But Mamó is happy, so thank you."

"You're welcome." She swiped a thumb over his lips, removing a light layer of red. "Shall we join Mamó at the head table?"

"Sure." He settled a hand in the sweet spot at the small of her back. "On the way you can explain your comment about a gentleman being interested in Mamó."

"I noticed a connection between her and a gentleman at the welcome party the other night—"

"No." He cut her off. "No noticing anything between her and any gentleman. Just turn your Spidey senses off."

She stopped abruptly, blocking his path. He almost tripped over his own feet to prevent himself from running into her.

Hands on hips, she slowly swung to face him. "You just can't help yourself can you?"

"What?"

"There you go, trying to control me. Worse, you're trying to control your grandmother, who deserves any chance at happiness fate hands her."

"I don't want you interfering."

"It's not 'Spidey senses,'" she informed him in icy tones. "It's a very real feeling about a connection between two people."

"Well, aim it elsewhere. Mamó is not interested."

"That's for Mamó to say, not you."

"I'm saying it for both of us." He stepped into her space, let her see he meant business. "Turn it off."

A flash of hurt went through her eyes before they frosted over in a blink. One red-tipped nail poked him in the chest, pushing him back.

"One: don't disrespect the matchmaking." Another poke. "Two: I'm here as a favor to you. Under protest, if you'll remember." Two pokes this time. "Three: you're just mad because I didn't run the idea by you first. I'd never do anything to hurt your grandmother. You're the one who will do that when she finds out our whole relationship is a sham and has been since the beginning."

She twirled on her stylish black heels, obviously planning to leave him in the dust.

He caught her arm. "Don't even *think* about telling her."

She glanced from his hand on her arm to his face. "It's good to know exactly what you think of me, Ray. For a while there you almost had me fooled that you were a decent guy. I thought I'd learned to see beyond a man's act."

He watched her throat work as she swallowed hard.

"Thanks for the reminder."

Stung, he dropped her arm. "Don't put me in league with that monster. I'm nothing like him."

"No?" She rubbed her arm. "You always have to be in control. You want to tell me what to do, who I can talk to, and what I can say. At least I can see it this time." A slight shiver shook her small frame and a hand went to her stomach. "Tell Mamó I'll be along in a few minutes. I'm going to talk to the facility director."

Again, she began to walk away. It struck him that he'd handled this badly. He'd never meant to hurt her. He just wanted to protect his grandmother.

"Lauren, wait." He moved quickly, blocking her escape. "I forgot four."

She nailed him with cold eyes. Who knew gold could cut so sharp?

"We're already done. I've been telling you that for days."

This time he let her go, his mind ticking over ways to fix this. He'd give her a few minutes to cool down. Let her do her business thing. It would help restore her sense of order. At least he hoped so.

Because he still saw that flash of raw hurt in her eyes. And it made him sick to his stomach that he was the one to put it there.

# CHAPTER SEVEN

THE ARGUMENT WITH Ray sent her scurrying for the restroom, the bitter taste of bile rising up her throat. Funny how her nausea often coincided with high emotions.

After she'd emptied her stomach, she liberated a few crackers from the buffet. Perched at a table on the edge of the room, she nibbled away and soon felt better. Well, her stomach felt better. Her emotions still felt thrashed.

Ray's behavior hurt. Did he really believe she'd put Mamó at risk? That she used her matchmaking gift to manipulate people?

That was his talent, not hers.

Wanting to avoid the aggravating man, she went in search of the facilities director. She thanked the plump brunette for allowing the last-minute additions to the decorations. The woman waved her off, saying she'd never seen the room look so pretty.

Lauren heard the same message again and again as she slowly made her way to the head table. And the cost had been minimal, as the flowers were recycled from a wedding earlier in the day. The five gentleman dancers accounted for the biggest expense, but it thrilled her to be able to add to Mamó's day.

Spending the night chained to Ray's side...? Not so enchanting.

He tried to pretend nothing had happened. She responded to his attempts at conversation with the briefest of responses. She wouldn't have responded at all except for Mamó. No need to draw her attention to their tiff.

After a while Ray excused himself and took off with his camera.

She didn't know who was more relieved to have him disappear behind the lens—him or her. Kyla slid into his vacant seat.

"You're my favorite person in the whole wide world." She squeezed Lauren's hand on the table. "The room is just stunning. And all the matrons are atwitter about the studs you lined up as dancing partners." She glanced over her shoulder at a couple of the men at the next table. "I'm kind of aglow myself."

Lauren laughed and nudged her new friend's shoulder. "The night's paid for. I say have fun."

"Really?" Kyla nibbled her bottom lip. "You wouldn't mind? You hired them for Mamó and her contemporaries."

"Of course I don't mind." Lauren assured her. "I want everyone to have a good time." She paused and pointed to the ninety-year-old woman chatting up Chad. "But you might not want to get between the men and Mrs. Harris."

Kyla snorted, then quickly clapped a hand over her mouth. "You're wicked." She leaned close. "To return the favor I'll warn you to stay clear of Old Man Tanner. He has wandering hands."

Pink-cheeked, Lauren asked for a refresher course on the names of the people she'd met the night before. "I'm usually good with names, but I was a tad distracted."

"I suppose news of your engagement might do that." With an understanding smile Kyla complied, adding bits of harmless gossip designed to help Lauren remember names.

Ellie broke in to steal Kyla away, muttering something about the cake.

When the music started Ray reappeared and asked her to dance. She declined. But she gladly accepted Chad when he returned Mamó to the table.

Ray's scowl as she walked off with Chad soothed her ravaged heart.

On the dance floor Lauren swayed lightly to a slow tune. Chad was charming and undemanding—two traits she particularly appreciated tonight.

Relaxing, she smiled at him. "You and your fellow dancers are a big hit."

"It's nice to be appreciated." He winked. "Actually, this is the first gig of this type I've heard of. I wouldn't mind if it caught on. It's nice to put a smile on a grandma's face. Is it true her grandson is *the* Ray Donovan?"

Lauren controlled a grimace. "Yes, he's the famous director. And it will thrill her to pieces if you ask her just like that."

"I like his movies. He's not afraid to take on hard core issues." His gaze traveled past her shoulder. "But obviously I'm a bigger fan of him than he is of me."

Lauren felt the weight of Ray's regard and knew Chad had just clashed gazes with her nemesis.

"Don't mind him. He's being a jerk, but it's not personal."

His gaze shifted past her again, then back down to her. "Do everyone a favor. Have pity. The guy is bringing the party down."

He'd barely finished speaking when a hand appeared on his shoulder and Ray asked to cut in.

Chad stepped back, bowed graciously, and disappeared into the crowd.

Lauren shifted her frown from one man to the other. *Men.*

"What's wrong?" Ray demanded as he pulled her close. "What did he do? Should I go after him?"

"No." She arched her eyebrows at him. Ray was the one who needed to apologize. The music stopped. She dropped her arms. "I want to return to the table."

Another ballad started. His arm tightened around her waist.

"Dance with me," he said. When she simply stared at him, he added, "Please. I want to apologize."

"Okay." She relented, sliding her arms up his hard chest to link her hands behind his head. "But only because your tantrum is marring Mamó's enjoyment of the party."

He made a rude noise in the back of his throat. "Hardly! Mamó barely knows I'm here. She's too busy dancing. Besides, I'm not the one walking away, dancing with other men."

Lauren closed her eyes. *Oh, goodness.* The very lack of emotion in Ray's voice revealed the depth of his upset. And it dawned on her that she was showing him up in front of the neighbors he already felt looked down on him.

*Dang.* She wasn't ready to give up being mad yet. But he didn't deserve another fifteen years of misery either. She relaxed in his hold and let him turn her around the floor.

"You're right. I'm sorry. I forgot your situation for a few minutes. I'll behave myself. But that doesn't mean you get to tell me what to do or mock my talent."

"Oh, I believe in it. Mamó has the same weird juju when it comes to babies. I just wish you could make it go away."

A hot tide of dread ran down Lauren's spine and a hard knot lodged in her throat. Praying that it didn't mean what she thought it meant, she gulped, then cleared her throat. "Mamó has a talent? Regarding babies? What? She can tell the sex?"

"The sex—and she's a walking early pregnancy test. She'll know someone's pregnant before they do. Made for some awkward moments growing up." He shook that off. "But we're talking about your talent. So, can you make it stop?"

*A walking early pregnancy test?* Nothing to worry about there...

Lauren propped her hands on her hips. "You're not usually so dense, Ray. I know you love your grandmother, and you're concerned. But you should be happy for her, not thinking of yourself." Enough. She'd let this go on too long. "If I'm not going to get my apology I'm returning to the table."

His hands tightened on her. "So hard tonight." He lifted her chin on the edge of his hand until she looked him in the eyes. His held regret. "I hurt you. I'm sorry."

The simplicity of his words arrowed right to her heart.

She lowered her eyes, unable to hold his gaze. Confronted with his sincerity, she was forced to face the truth. Her anger acted as a shield. Otherwise she'd too easily fall into his arms again. Especially at the party.

Every time they'd hooked up it had been at a festive event of some sort, starting with Thanksgiving at his Malibu mansion last November.

She'd gone with him to set up the poker table in the loft. They'd started arguing over nothing, he'd kissed her, and the electricity between them had flared out of control. The open loft overlooked the living room, where her father and brother had been watching football, so Ray had dragged her around the corner into the first room they stumbled across—which had happened to be the laundry room.

To this day she couldn't do the laundry without blushing.

"Lauren?" He breathed her name against her temple. "Am I forgiven?"

"Oh. Of course." She bowed her head. "I may have overreacted a bit."

"No." He pulled back to see her better. "I'm the one at fault. I know you'd never hurt Mamó. And you have no control over the attraction you sense. It's just—"

Suddenly he swung Lauren around until they had a clear view of Mamó, dancing with an older gentleman with a full head of gray hair, a Van Dyke beard and mustache. "It's George Meade, isn't it? He's been sniffing around her all night."

Her stomach took longer to catch up than the rest of her. Lauren leaned against Ray and drew in some deep breaths.

"Hey…" A big hand cradled her head to him. "Are you okay?"

"Just a little dizzy," she assured him.

Regaining her composure, she created some distance between them.

"I know it freaks you out, thinking about her with a man, but having someone to focus on in her life besides you and your potential offspring might be the answer to your problem."

"Huh," he responded, his gaze focused across the room again. "I'm right, aren't I? It's Meade."

"I'm not saying." Lauren refused to throw the poor man to this predator stalking him. From the corner of her eye, she saw Mamó circling the floor in George Meade's arms. The faint glow of their connection reached Lauren across the distance. "Let Mamó have her evening."

"So it *is* him." Ray released her, his intent clear.

She grabbed his arm before he took two steps. "If you interrupt them I'm leaving."

He froze. "You said you'd behave."

"How I behave won't matter if I'm gone."

Taking her hand, he drew her to the edge of the dance floor. "I just want to talk to him. I'll only be a minute." He turned toward his quarry.

"I won't stop until I'm back in Hollywood," she warned him.

He pivoted in his Italian leather shoes to face her. "You wouldn't?"

She crossed her arms and pinned him with a glare.

"That's just mean."

"You have no idea." Her fingers bit into the fabric of his jacket as she pulled him further away from the dancing. "This is your grandmother's birthday party. I'm not going to let you embarrass her in front of her friends."

"You mean her *man* friend." He scowled.

"Him most of all." Aware of the hard muscle under her fingers, she dropped her hand.

Turmoil roiled inside him. She felt the surge of emotion as much as she saw it storm across his features.

"Just because I sense a connection it doesn't mean anything will come of it. It's up to them to act on it. Or not. But if you interfere you'd better believe I will be on the next plane out of here."

For just a second panic flared in his blue eyes. "You wouldn't really leave me alone with these people?"

She blinked at him, totally unprepared for his reaction even though it confirmed her earlier revelation. The flash of vulnerability exposed how difficult this trip was for him.

She took his hand. "Ray, these people are your family, your friends. They all care about you."

His face shuttered. "They like to claim they know me." He glanced around. "But none of them really does. They care because I'm famous and because of Mamó."

"They could hate you for the same reasons, but they don't."

She debated for a moment about her next move. Her confession might freak him out more than reassure him. She straightened her shoulders and went for it.

"Listen, the same vibe that allows me to see a connection between a couple also lets me pick up on high-level emotions. And the overall feeling in this room is positive—to the point it overwhelms everything else."

He stared at her for a moment, then cupped her cheek and drew her to him for a brief kiss.

"What you're feeling is for Mamó," he said.

"Yes," she agreed. "But I haven't noticed any malice or envy around you. And I think I would." She laid her head on his chest, felt the steady beat of his heart. "Just because they don't know all your secrets it doesn't mean they don't care."

And, oh, how she wished the sentiment didn't strike so close to home.

"Ray...Lauren." Kyla joined them. "Look who I have. This is Lulu, my goddaughter—isn't she beautiful?"

Lauren pulled back, but Ray kept his arm around her waist. She focused on the baby in Kyla's arms.

She held a tiny little girl with dark button eyes, pink bow lips, and short dark curls. Lulu couldn't be more than five months old and she melted Lauren's heart.

Her throat closed up at the thought she'd soon hold a baby of her own.

"Oh, my goodness. She's so sweet." She itched to hold the baby, but Ray beat her to it.

"She's a heartbreaker." He plucked the infant from his cousin. "Aren't you, my beauty?" He held her with confidence and ease, his comfort in handling the child obvious.

Lulu grinned, her bow mouth a perfect O, flashing toothless gums and innocent joy.

"Ah..."

Lauren and Kyla echoed each other, which caused them to laugh.

"She likes you." Lauren ran her finger over the petal-soft skin of the baby's hand. Lulu promptly wrapped her fingers around Lauren's digit.

Kyla snorted. "*All* women love him. Not even a five-month-old is immune to his charm." She held up a camera. "Her mama wants a picture." She stood back and clicked a shot of Lauren, Ray, and Lulu. "Thanks."

"What about Mama?" Ray asked. "We should get one with her, too."

Kyla beamed. "She would totally love that. I told her you'd go for it— Oh, my lord, *no*! Those little stinkers are going for the cake. Be right back." She took off at a trot, a fierce glint in her eyes.

"Oops." Ray's gaze followed his cousin's retreat. "Wouldn't want to be one of those boys."

"No."

Lauren couldn't take her eyes off Ray. Watching him with the little girl had charmed her more than she would have believed. He was so natural with the child. Actually, it surprised her. She would have expected just the opposite.

"You're very good with her."

"I'm into kids," he confessed. "I'm godfather to my assistant's one-year-old boy. I love when he brings him to the house. We play catch."

"Catch with a one-year-old?"

"Okay, you got me." He grinned. "We play chase the ball. But it's fun."

Lulu waved her arms and yammered a mouthful of noises. Ray bounced her in his arms.

"Don't worry, sweetness, we haven't forgotten you. Do you want to hold her?"

Lauren nodded and he passed the child to her. She gathered the tiny girl into her arms. How light she felt, yet warm and cuddly. "Well, hello, Lulu."

She received a big grin just like Ray had got. The precious moment lifted her spirits. She held a miracle in her arms. And soon she'd hold her own miracle.

Lulu waved her plump arms and latched onto Lauren's hoop earring. "Oh. Ouch!"

"I've got it." Ray gently held Lulu's arm and worked her fingers free of the gold hoop. His eyes were laughing as he looked down at Lauren. "For someone so small, she's got a good grip."

"She's perfect." Lauren bounced her gently. "But we really should find her mother and return her."

"Just one dance first." Ray wrapped his arms around her waist, swung the three of them onto the dance floor, and set up a mellow sway.

"You really need to learn to wait for an answer," she chided him. But her reprimand lacked heat. "I think she's tired. Her eyes are closing."

"Oh, yeah, she'll be out soon." His unreadable gaze lingered on her and the child. "You look good with a baby in your arms."

"Hmm?" She stalled, her mind flashing to his child in her womb.

It took all her concentration not to miss a step. She'd envisioned a life with just her child and her—based on his single jet-set lifestyle she'd figured he wouldn't want a child in his life. Certainly not disrupting his home. Seeing him with Lulu had put those notions into question.

"You looked pretty good yourself. Surprised me, really."

"They're just little people."

Not really…

"So, you plan to have a few kids of your own someday?" She held her breath, waiting for his answer.

His body tensed and he didn't respond right away, his gaze focused over her left shoulder. "Maybe," he finally allowed. "Never say never, right?"

Breath rushed back into her lungs. What kind of nonanswer was that?

"I want kids," she shared, watching for a reaction. "At least two…maybe three."

He zeroed in on her, heat flaring in his pale eyes, moving over her face and then over the child in her arms. Her body reacted to him, warming under his regard. He lowered his head and she angled hers, anticipating a kiss.

"She's asleep," he whispered.

"Asleep?"

Lauren blinked. In the space of those two seconds her mind had shut off and her body had taken over. It took a moment for her brain synapses to start firing again.

"The baby. Oh, right."

"We should get her back to her mother."

"Yes. You definitely owe her a picture for taking her child hostage."

"I'm putting the blame for that right where it belongs."

He directed her through the other dancers with a hand at the small of her back. "Squarely on Kyla's shoulders."

Lauren shook her head. "Is anything *ever* your fault?"

"Rarely."

"Ha!" *Of course not.* "Why do you say that?"

"Mostly because I don't play the blame game. It's not constructive. I plan and I fix. I provide good directions, and when something goes wrong I come up with a new plan. It's pretty close to the way I've seen you run your events company."

It was *exactly* the way she and Tori ran By Arrangement.

"I'm always excited when an event comes together without a hitch. But I confess it's exhilarating when we pull off an event that's been problematic."

"Right. It's more about the process than the end result."

"Exactly."

Listening to him made her realize how alike their careers were. He created movies and she created events. His were caught on tape and hers were more in the moment, but they both required careful direction and the ability to adjust. "That's what I enjoy most about being an event coordinator—it's an organic experience."

"You've discovered my secret. Now I'll have to kill you." He waved at Kyla, who stood beside a larger version of Lulu. "Or marry you."

"What—? Huh?" She clutched the baby so hard she woke up and squealed. "Shh, baby. I'm sorry." She glared at Ray. "That wasn't funny."

"Oh, but it was." Laughter danced in his eyes. His lips softly touched hers. "Remind me not to propose again while you're holding a baby."

# CHAPTER EIGHT

"Mmm. It smells wonderful in here." Mamó strolled over to a lush chair in soft teal and sat. "I might have to take some of whatever that is home." She indicated the seat next to her. "Come. Sit. Ray said he'd see us here at eleven. We're a few minutes early."

Lauren took in the elegant reception area of the exclusive day spa. Ray had swept them away from Queens early that morning, treating them to breakfast at the Plaza before dashing off to a meeting with the mayor. The spa had been a short walk up Fifth Avenue in the thirty-four-degree weather. Mamó had called it pleasant.

*Pleasant?* Wasn't thirty-two freezing? Thank heavens for the red leather coat.

"Good morning. Welcome to Nouveaux Vous."

A beautiful redhead appeared at the front desk. She wore a classic black dress that contrasted with her milky complexion. Her make-up was flawless, not a freckle in sight. Her serene expression fit perfectly with the elegant pale teal and cream decor.

"Fern Donovan and Lauren Randall?"

"Yes. We're meeting my fiancé here."

How odd did that sound? Apparently they did have an appointment, though Lauren was surprised to hear her name. She and Ray were supposed to be going siting for a movie scheduled to start filming toward the end of the year. Finding out Ray had made an appointment for her was disappointing. She'd been jazzed at the prospect of seeing some of this famous city.

"We have you both listed for a massage, facial, and glamor. Mr. Donovan arranged for you to have your sessions together. Rene and Kim are available when you're ready. May I get you coffee or water while you wait?"

Mamó shook her head.

"No, thank you." Lauren checked her phone. "No message from him. We're going to wait for a few minutes," she told the receptionist.

Aware this was the moment she'd been dreading, Lauren settled next to Mamó in a lobby chair.

Since learning of Mamó's ability to tell when a woman was pregnant, Lauren had anxiously anticipated a confrontation with the older woman. Until now they'd been in company or on the move. She could put it off no longer.

The other woman spoke first, patting Lauren's hand on the armrest between them. "I want to thank you for your gifts. There was no need for you to bother—just having you here is such a joy to me. But the extra decor and having the gentlemen there to dance with was a treat beyond telling."

"I'm happy it added to your day," Lauren responded honestly.

"Oh, it made my year. My friends had such a grand time. No one will top this event for years."

"I'm glad you had a good time." Lauren smiled at Mamó's joy. Then she sobered. "You know, don't you?" She didn't look at Mamó but at the placid seascape on the far wall.

Mamó didn't respond right away. Then her hand covered Lauren's and she squeezed. "It's your news to share. I respect that."

"Ray doesn't know," Lauren said.

"I've gathered that." There was no judgment in Mamó's voice, just curiosity.

"It's hard to see him as a father."

Or it had been before she'd watched him cradle little Lulu in his arms. The sight of the big, strong man confidently holding the precious infant had changed everything. Or it could change nothing. She needed time to re-evaluate.

"He's always been good with kids. I think that's what hurt him most in the breakup." Mamó's hand shook and she pulled it back into her lap. She twined her fingers together until the knuckles showed white.

Lauren stilled. This must be the incident Ray had referenced. "The breakup?"

"He must have told you? It's the one time I truly regretted my talent. But I couldn't let him say his vows without knowing the truth."

"No, of course not," she soothed.

Vows? Questions ricocheted through her head. She wanted to press Mamó for answers but refrained. The older woman was already distressed by the conversation. Better to calm her down before Ray arrived. She'd put the questions to him at a more appropriate time.

Mamó's unusual talent might have pushed up Lauren's agenda to tell Ray, but it didn't change her concerns over his emotional availability to his child. She needed to know about the past before she could make a decision about the future.

"Honesty is important to Ray," Lauren reassured her.

"That's what I told myself even though I knew he'd leave." Mamó wrung her hands. "It was for the best. He's an important man now."

"I have the feeling Ray would be important whatever he did."

"Probably." Mamó nodded. "But he saw no future for himself here. I had to tell him."

"It was the right thing to do."

Curiosity was killing Lauren, but it wouldn't be fair to

pump Mamó. The story needed to come from Ray. Just as the news of their child needed to come from her.

"I'm going to tell him."

"Of course, dear. I won't say anything," Mamó assured her. "Unless I'm asked, I've learned to keep what I know to myself. Well, most of the time."

The shop door opened and Ray walked in on a blast of "pleasant" air. His presence filled the space along with his broad shoulders. Lauren hopped up and he greeted her with a kiss on the cheek. And then he bent to kiss Mamó's powder-dusted cheek. For a man who prized his privacy so strongly he was demonstrative. She'd pretty much given up on the no touching rule. The man just couldn't keep his hands, or his lips, to himself.

And apparently she couldn't keep to her side of the bed. She'd woken up wrapped around him again this morning. This time she'd got caught—literally—while she'd been trying to unfurl herself from him. He had turned over and met her nose to nose.

She'd refused to admit to disappointment when he had merely wished her good morning with a brief peck on the forehead before bounding from the bed to hit the bathroom first.

Oddly, sleeping with him seemed to suit the baby, because her morning queasiness had all but disappeared.

She'd always considered his bid for privacy to have stemmed from arrogance, but now she knew him better she thought it might be more a matter of self-defense. It was something to think about.

"Listen, babe, there's been a change of plans. The master of the Port Authority isn't available tomorrow, so I'm meeting with him today and viewing the docks. That's going to be a cold, dirty trek I'm sure you have no interest in. Instead I booked you matching spa treatments with Mamó. Is that okay?"

Dirty docks or a facial? No-brainer. "Sure."

"Good." He kissed her again, this time on the lips, a gesture of simple affection. Clearly his mind was elsewhere. "I'll pick you up at three and we'll go shopping."

"Shopping?" She was not letting him buy her another thing.

"Yes, the mayor invited me to a black tie reception tonight. I told him I'd be escorting my two best ladies."

"Ray—" The protest had barely passed her lips when a well-attired man with black hair opened the door and nodded at Ray.

"Sorry, Dynamite, I have to go. We'll talk later."

And then he was gone and the redhead was back. Lauren sighed and shared a glance with Mamó, who shrugged.

"He's a busy man."

*Yeah, right.* But Lauren didn't push it. "Shall we go get pampered?"

"Yes—and we should buy some of that lovely-smelling lotion. I'm sure Ray would want us to have some."

A smile tugged at the corner of Lauren's mouth because she had no doubt he would. "Yes, we really need some lotion."

Four hours later Lauren followed Mamó from the spa feeling refreshed and revitalized. The massage and facial had worked all the toxins and tension from her body. The beauty regimen had pampered her in a whole new way, leaving her feeling beautiful and eager to show off her pretty new look.

She really must schedule a spa day for her and Tori post-honeymoon.

Mamó had a real glow about her, too. Though some of that might have been due to the call she'd taken from Ellie. She'd made plans for dinner back in Queens and Lauren got the impression George Meade might be involved. Seemed Mamó wanted to showcase *her* new glamor, too.

Lauren didn't push for details. What she didn't know she couldn't spill to Ray.

Bright shafts of sunshine fought through the cloud cover and high-rises to warm the afternoon pedestrians. A limousine stood double-parked at the curb. Ray stepped out as they approached.

He flattered Mamó on how lovely she looked, accepted the news she wanted to bow out of the reception with good grace, and sent her off in the limo, suggesting she use the car service to collect her friends for dinner.

"She always gets a kick out of her neighbors' reaction when she comes and goes in a limousine. She'll be extra excited to give them a ride."

Enchanted with his obvious affection for his grandmother, Lauren hooked her arm through his. "Today she feels beautiful and special. You did good."

Satisfaction showed in the form of a smirk. "Good. There's still a sadness about her, but Ellie says she's been better the last few days." He waved down a passing cab. "How was she today?"

"Fine. It was a mellow day. And she seems excited about tonight."

"Good." He nodded and helped her into the waiting taxi. "Bloomingdales," he directed the driver.

Lauren settled into her seat without argument. She'd already decided to treat herself to a new dress for the reception and as a souvenir of the trip. By Arrangement's success over the past year certainly allowed for a little extravagance—which reminded her: the designer of Tori's wedding dress had a loft in New York. Lauren loved her work.

She scrolled through her contacts, made a quick call, and then asked Ray to change their destination.

"I'm glad you're getting into the spirit of tonight's adventure." He swept a loose tendril of hair behind her ear.

"Hmm?" She relaxed against him. "Are we having an adventure?"

"Yes. This is our first official date."

"So it is." Tipping her head back, she eyed his profile. He appeared pleased with himself. "There's likely to be press at this event. How do you want to handle it?" she asked.

"Word of our engagement is out. I already got asked about it a couple of times today."

"What did you say?"

"That I wasn't answering questions. But I'll make a brief statement tonight." He picked up her hand, threaded his fingers through hers. "I'm sorry you got dragged into a lie."

"Thank you, but it's not your fault."

"I had my team put together a news release. I'll show it to you at the hotel. It includes who you are, when we met, how long we've dated and details currently known about the wedding."

"You have a team?"

"I do. Besides my assistant there's my manager, a publicist, a project manager, an accountant, and—to my shame and at my assistant's insistence—a stylist."

She laughed and slapped his knee. "You do *not* have a stylist."

"Only during awards season. Which reminds me—will you be my date for the awards ceremony this weekend?"

"Walk the red carpet with you?"

Her eyes popped and she sucked in a breath before she got herself under control. The awards were a big deal for Ray this year. They were equally important to her career.

"I'm working that night."

"If we make an announcement, everyone will expect you to attend with me."

"By Arrangement is handling Obsidian Studio's after-party." She rubbed her thumb over his knuckle. "It's been our goal since we focused our business in Hollywood to cater a post-awards ball."

"And I'm betting it will be *the* party to beat this year. People are still talking about the job you ladies did for Obsidian at the Hollywood Hills Film Festival. Couldn't you keep an eye on things from the perspective of being my date?"

His request went totally against her work ethic. She shouldn't even be here this week, but preparing and over-seeing the biggest event of her career. Work had become her savior, her solace. She took comfort in the discipline and control necessary to pull off a spectacular event.

But with a baby under her heart and a major life deci-sion to make regarding her child's future her mind couldn't focus on work. She owed it to herself, to her baby, and to Ray to take the time to make the most informed decision she could. In the meantime, twice daily updates from her assistant kept her sane on the work front.

She recalled Mamó's mention of vows and realized there was so much about Ray she didn't know. Dates were meant to help a couple get to know each other better. So that was what she would do. Enjoy the night, learn more about Ray, and maybe get some answers about his past.

Whatever his reservations about his old neighborhood, he hadn't deserted his community. On her way to the re-stroom at the community center last night she'd spied a plaque posted in gratitude to Raymond Patrick Donovan for the donation of a gymnasium and pool.

Dated seven years ago, the timing of the donation matched his first huge success—a film about a wounded veteran saving a small town from a corrupt mayor. He'd blended drama and action into a brilliant display of brav-ery, sacrifice, and justice that had provided moviegoers with an emotional and visually satisfying experience. The film had made Ray's name a household word—he'd swept the awards that year, and gone on to become part of the Hollywood elite.

And Ray had handed a cool million to his old neighborhood.

"I'll think about it. Let's get through tonight first."

"Deal. We're here." He climbed from the cab, glanced up at the building. "She's stretching the limits of the garment district, here."

"That doesn't really mean anything to me," she said as she joined him. "Did you see Tori's wedding dress? Fabulous. She found it at a small boutique on Rodeo Drive, and of course she had to call the designer to rave about it. The two of them are now email buddies."

Inside, the receptionist directed them to the third floor. Eve Gardner met them at the door.

"Lauren, I'm so glad you called." The slim blond greeted them in her showroom. "I've seen pictures of the wedding. Tori was absolutely stunning—you must share all the details."

"I will, but first let me say your dress was the jewel in her day. I've never seen her look more beautiful."

"As a designer I can promise you *she* made the dress—not the other way around. My phone hasn't stopped ringing all week." She laughed lightly, looking a little shell shocked. "I should have paid her to wear the dress!"

Lauren squeezed her hand. "You deserve the recognition. It was a stunning dress. I'm hoping you might have something for me." She introduced Ray. "We're going to a reception for the mayor tonight."

"Tonight?" Eve's eyes widened as she recognized Ray, but she quickly recovered and pulled Lauren further into her shop, introducing the two of them to her assistant, Christy. "What type of affair is it?"

"Black tie."

"Hmm, what are you? A size five? I think I have a couple of items you might like."

Eve invited Lauren and Ray to sit and then disappeared into the back. Christy offered them refreshments and then followed Eve.

Lauren sat on a dove-gray tufted sofa while Ray roamed the showroom. The white walls provided an excellent showcase for the life-sized framed prints of celebrities and models in Eve's designs. Several racks around the room held vibrantly hued garments.

"Nice." Ray stopped in front of a print of a high-profile actress in a midnight-blue dress on which the bodice consisted of strategically placed bands artfully woven across the breasts and throat while the skirt fell in a straight sheath to the floor.

"That's showing too much skin for me."

He turned back to her, arms crossed over his chest. "You'd be stunning in something like this."

She shook her blond head. "I should have told her something conservative would be best. Preferably in black."

"Absolutely not. Tonight isn't a job. It's fun. You need a dress to play in."

"I won't be working this event," she agreed, mimicking him by crossing her arms over her breasts. "But you will. I need to respect that."

"Dynamite, in my business the more skin you show the better."

"Yes, but I'm only visiting your world. In my world I can wear the dress again at an event I *will* be working."

"If you don't have the guts all you have to do is say so." He strolled over and dropped down beside her, his arm resting on the back of the sofa behind her.

"I don't have the guts."

No need to bluff. And she wouldn't let him dare her into wearing something she couldn't be comfortable in. That was Tori—not her. Classy and conservative suited her just fine.

"Okay," he said easily, tracing a finger over her ear,

making her shiver. The man was always *touching*. "But you have the body for it. Just so you know."

"You're not supposed to be thinking of my body. Remember? It's one of the rules we discussed."

"I thought you gave up on those rules?"

"No. What made you think that?" She should never have let him get away with the constant touching. It gave him the wrong idea.

"I don't know. Possibly the fact I've woken up with you curled around me the last couple of nights."

Heat rose in her cheeks. The hope that he'd slept through her nighttime wanderings ended at this embarrassing revelation. Of course she knew it had been a futile hope.

"That doesn't count," she bluffed. "We can't control what we do while we're sleeping."

He leaned close, bringing the scent of man and spice with him. He whispered in her ear. "That's not what you said the other night."

"Yes…well…" He smelled so good she'd lost her train of thought. *Oh, yeah.* "The point is the rules are in full force. And you're breaking them."

"Wrong. The rules say no unnecessary touching. I can admire all I want."

*No.* He had to stop. His admiring and his touching were chipping away at her resolve. She'd agreed to their date tonight, to get to know him better. But already she felt her control slipping. Being the sole focus of his attention might be more than she could handle.

"Your admiring is making it hard to breathe." She put a finger in the middle of his chest and pushed. "Behave yourself."

"Okay." He settled back into his place, but didn't remove his arm from behind her. "But you're forgetting the security cameras. Touching is totally within our limits."

Of course he'd be aware of the cameras. Short of pleading, she only had one other option. A good threat.

"Go ahead—have your fun now. Risk putting me in a bad mood for tonight, when I'll be wearing a sexy dress and sipping a nice wine."

"Good point."

His blue eyes narrowed, showing her he'd caught her meaning. The gleam in those eyes sent a message too. He knew he bothered her. And he planned to put that knowledge to good use later.

He gave her ear a tug and pulled out his phone. "I'll just return a few texts."

"You do that." She reached for her purse. Actually, it was a good time to check her own messages. All was well at By Arrangement. Her mom was still waiting for a full explanation. And no word yet from Tori.

"Here we go." Eve returned, Christy on her heels, with a handful of dresses in her arms. "Come with me. I found a lovely cobalt gown perfect for your skin tone."

"Wait." Ray waved his phone. "How long will this take?"

Lauren stared at him blankly, then turned to Eve.

The designer shrugged. "As long as it takes."

Lauren nodded.

He stood, looking back and forth between them as if expecting something more. "Right. I have something to take care of. I'll be back for you."

"No."

"You want me to wait?" He lifted his phone to impart his response.

"No."

He went still and lifted a brown eyebrow, waiting for her direction.

Okay, she had to admit it was heady stuff. Except for her rules, she'd been following his lead for this whole trip. It was nice to have a little power. It might only be over travel plans, but she'd take it.

"You go ahead. I'll catch a cab and meet you back at the hotel."

They had decided to stay in the city for the night, in the suite Ray had originally booked for them.

"Okay." He advised the person on the other end of the phone he'd be there shortly. Then he came over, kissed her hard, and headed out, taking her hard-won power with him.

But not for long.

She turned to Eve. "I hope the cobalt is sexy."

# CHAPTER NINE

THE BLUE FABRIC clung to Lauren's curves. A fitted bodice flowed into two straps that both went over one shoulder, creating an asymmetrical keyhole. The straps narrowed to two-inch strips spanning her bare back. The skirt hugged her hips before falling in a straight line to the floor.

Ray sipped a well-balanced whiskey as he half listened to the mayor talking about the summit underway at the United Nations. Undoubtedly it was a worthy endeavor, but Ray found his attention held by two blue straps—or, more specifically, by the creamy skin they didn't cover. His fingers itched to touch.

A few members of the society press were covering the event out front. They'd lit up like kids on Christmas morning when they'd spied him and Lauren. Made him glad he had the press statement ready.

Lauren had handled the congratulations and intrusive questions well, but her poise had failed to disguise the tremors running through her body—especially when an idiot had demanded to know if she was pregnant.

Ray had wanted to plant his fist in the man's mouth. Instead he'd shut the questions off and moved her inside. They'd made it through the informal procession line with no further incident.

He enjoyed having her at his side. She neither preened nor disappeared. Nor did she defer to him, but treated him as he imagined she treated all her dates—as an equal.

Which influenced those around them, easing the burden of his celebrity.

It was a treat he took full advantage of for over an hour. Difficult to enjoy an event when people feared approaching you or made the conversation all about you. This room held important men who wielded real power. Even casual discussions rippled with nuances of bigger things.

It was almost enough to engage his whole attention. But there was always a part of him aware of Lauren, whether she stood at his side or had wandered a few feet away in a breakaway discussion.

Something about the woman got to him.

He'd earned a reputation for being a hardcore bachelor long ago because he guarded his privacy and made it clear to all his companions that they could expect nothing more from him than a good time and a fond farewell.

Generally he stuck to two dating pools when he wanted female company: women in the industry but behind the camera, because they were familiar with what it meant to be in the limelight, or women unconnected with the industry, because he didn't have to worry that they were trying to further their careers.

Lauren straddled the line, giving him the best of both worlds. He was comfortable with her—which might freak him out except for the sizzling chemistry between them.

He wouldn't be used because of his occupation. He wouldn't be used, period. Being seen as a meal ticket and an escape out of the neighborhood had taught him that harsh lesson before he'd ever made it big.

And the price had been the life of his child.

On his wedding day he had truly understood that anybody could be driven to kill. If not for Mamó he might well have crossed the line.

He shook off the memory. Not the time. Not the place. His fingers itched.

Lauren thought she was safe, standing in deep discussion with the mayor's wife. But she'd set the rules. He could only touch her in public. So, actually, she'd chosen the place. It was only fair he should choose the time.

He'd been very restrained so far. From the stunning moment when she'd stepped from her room at the hotel, through the limo ride to the reception, to having her by his side through the barrage of introductions.

His patience was at an end.

"Are we boring you, Ray?"

Bob, the governor of New Jersey, clapped him on the back, drawing his attention back to the group.

"I know you're not working tonight, but I'll admit I was hoping for a chance to talk to you about using the great state of New Jersey in one of your films."

"I'm afraid I'm not very familiar with New Jersey, other than flying into the airport."

"Well, I'm happy to rectify that. I can arrange a tour at your convenience."

"Thanks, but my time is limited on this trip, and I have several locations to site tomorrow. I expect it to take most of the day."

"I've put an aide and a limousine at his disposal for the day," the mayor interjected.

"A helicopter would be more efficient, and then you could add a couple of Jersey sights."

"A helicopter?" Ray mused, liking the idea. Liking the idea of smoothing his hand over lotion-scented skin even more. Lauren might get a kick out of an aerial tour.

"Have your assistant contact my office with your schedule." Bob pulled out a card. "And I'll have a bird ready and waiting."

"Come on, Bob," the mayor interposed. "Are you trying to steal my revenue stream?" He was only half joking.

Lauren's laugh tinkled on the air, the sound energizing Ray.

Bob shrugged big shoulders. "I just want to show Ray,

here, the diversity of my beautiful state so he can keep us in mind for future ventures."

The mayor harrumphed.

"Thanks, Bob," Ray said. He flicked the card. "My assistant will be in touch. Gentlemen, it's been a pleasure."

"Running off so soon?" the mayor protested, then followed Ray's gaze to where the women chatted a few feet away. A look of admiration chased away the touch of irritation in his eyes. "Ah. I understand. Congratulations, by the way. You're a lucky man."

"Indeed."

He nodded to the men and strolled the short distance to Lauren's side, shaking off the odd combination of pride and anger at the way the other man had eyed Lauren.

He wasn't usually territorial. Then again he didn't usually have a temporary fiancée either. That had to be it.

His fingers connected with the skin of her lower back and he sighed. Satisfaction and desire replaced all other emotions.

Lauren instantly acknowledged him, looking up and back. She continued her conversation but settled into his touch.

"It's really not that difficult to up the interest factor of an event," she explained to the cluster of ladies. "It can be as simple as having a signature cocktail or adding visual props."

"These affairs always look the same," a white-haired matron said, while fingering the diamonds at her neck.

"That usually happens when it's left up to a hotel. Understated elegance is a classic, so it's often the default mode." She responded calmly, as if her audience wasn't sending furtive glances his way.

"What would you have done differently tonight?" the mayor's wife asked.

"We often work with the client to come up with a theme. Lacking that, I'd switch things up. Flowers are a standard, but instead of roses I might have gone with something more exotic. A tropical feel in the middle of winter would be welcomed by most. And I might have replaced a few of the round tables with a conversation area of sofas and chairs."

A hum of approval came from the group.

Lauren shrugged gracefully. "My sister is the truly creative half of our team."

"Ladies," Ray broke in, "I'm going to steal Lauren away. We have reservations for a late supper."

"How romantic," the matron announced. "Enjoy these early days, dear. It's never quite the same once you've said your vows."

"And Marian should know," one of the others volunteered.

"Yes," Marian agreed with a trill of laughter. "Walter is my third husband."

"Let's give Walter something to think about, shall we?" Ray lifted Marian's diamond-laden hand to his mouth and pressed a kiss to the back of her fingers.

Marian flushed pink, her delight in being singled out bright in her smile.

"Ladies…" He winked and led Lauren away.

Watching the world spin away before her sent Lauren's stomach rolling. Not because of the baby this time, but the dizzying ride in a glass elevator. Placing a hand on her belly, she turned away from the rising view.

"You okay?" Ray wrapped an arm around her waist and pulled her close.

"Vertigo." She leaned against him, took comfort in the caress of his hand on her back. "Better now. Thanks."

The elevator opened on the forty-seventh floor. Ray gestured for her to exit. She did so, but questioned him.

"You said we had reservations for a late supper. I thought we were headed for the rooftop restaurant?"

"It's been a long day. I ordered in." He used a card key to let them into the lounge area of their suite. "I hope you don't mind?"

"No, but I'm disappointed. I was looking forward to relaxing while taking in the rooftop view. New York keeps beckoning, yet I've only seen a slice of the Big Apple."

This was exactly the type of highhanded behavior she found annoying.

"Sorry." Loosening his tie, he bent to kiss her on the top of her head. "I've had enough of being a spectacle today. I had them set the table up by the window, so the view should be nearly the same."

"Oh…" Now she felt bad. She hadn't considered how being "on" all the time must get tiring for him.

Feeling the quiet of the room embrace her, she admitted it was a stellar option.

"Good thinking. What did you order for us?"

"Lobster, steak, a full range of sides and desserts." At the dining table he began lifting lids on dome-covered dishes. "I wanted you to have a choice."

"How thoughtful." And it was. Her mood improved. "This looks delicious."

Ray handed her a plate, took one for himself, and they served themselves. She chose both lobster and a small piece of steak, with asparagus and tender red potatoes.

"How's the vertigo?" Ray's concerned gaze ran over her features as he held her chair. "Would you like me to pull the table away from the window?"

Touched, she smiled her appreciation. "No, I'll be fine. It was the motion combined with the view that got to me. Here the table blocks the feet-to-skyline view, so I should be all right. But I think I'll skip the wine, just to be safe."

Finding ways to decline alcohol and caffeine were getting harder and harder.

She set her plate down and allowed him to seat her. "This is lovely."

New York in all its glistening glory was spread out before them. High-rises and bridges threaded together with streets of lights. She recognized the Empire State Building and Ray pointed out several other landmarks.

"Where's Queens?" she asked.

"You can't see it from here. Wrong angle." But he pointed out the boroughs they *could* see amidst the myriad buildings. Even from this height and distance the city's flow and movement reached her. New York was a living, breathing metropolis unlike any place else she'd ever seen.

He told her about his day at the docks, making her laugh with his dry sense of humor. She refrained from boring him with details of her day at the spa, assuring him instead that it had been relaxing. "Not as relaxing as this, though."

A gleam appeared in his eyes. He reached over and threaded long fingers through her smaller ones. His touch soothed and aroused.

"I know what you mean. It feels like forever since we've been alone."

Yes. She got that. And the fact she'd missed him was as surprising as it was true.

She felt as if she'd been on edge for days. They'd been together almost constantly, but rarely on their own. To all intents and purposes they were truly alone for the first time since leaving Hollywood. Well, except for the time they spent together in his small bedroom—which was not relaxing in the least.

Baby might enjoy sleeping in Daddy's arms, but Mama found the whole experience nerve-racking.

Tonight the mood was intimate, yet mellow. The amazing view and the delectable food were too good to ruin with bad vibes. The ease between them presented the perfect opportunity to address something bothering her.

Mamó had mentioned vows in connection with Ray, and something to do with a pregnancy. It wasn't hard to connect the dots, but she didn't work well with supposition. She liked solid facts. Much less room for misunderstandings.

The one time she had allowed herself to have faith in her emotions she'd sunk deep in an emotionally damaging relationship. Some—Tori—might call it abusive. Lauren's pride argued that she'd pulled out before it had reached that stage.

The point was she'd learned a tough lesson: not to let her heart lead her head. Especially now she had a child to think of.

"Can I ask you a personal question?"

"Sure. We're engaged—at least for a few more days."

Uh, no, they weren't. But they *were* going to be parents. She figured that gave her a right to know. So she'd run with his permission.

"Have you been married before?"

He stared at her with an unreadable expression for a long moment, until she wondered if he'd answer her after all. Then he stood, pulled her to her feet by their joined fingers and led her to the large, plush couch.

"If we're going to get into something deep, let's get comfortable."

He sat and drew her down next to him, never letting go of her. And still he didn't elaborate. He played with her fingers, his gazed locked on their entwined digits, their hands perched on his hard thigh, because he'd allowed no space between them.

"I suppose someone mentioned it to you at the party?" Bitterness edged his response. "Fifteen years and four major industry awards and I *still* haven't lived it down."

Okay, that didn't sound like a denial. Then again, she'd never heard of marriage referred to as "it" either.

"So you *were* married?"

"No."

An odd sense of relief slid through her.

Ridiculous, of course. And unfounded. It would be unhealthy for a man his age never to have been involved in a committed relationship. So he preferred to be discreet? That didn't mean he didn't have a private life. Or that he didn't care for the women he spent time with.

Okay, so their interaction had been purely physical, with nothing more than a fake engagement to indicate any sense of depth. She'd be a fool to assume all his relationships were so shallow.

But he hadn't cared enough to get married. She supposed that meant something. She hoped hearing his history might give her the answers she needed.

He'd been quiet while she stewed. Brooding himself?

"Painful memories?" She squeezed his fingers and leaned her head on his shoulder.

"Yeah." It was almost a grunt.

"You don't have to talk about it if you don't want to," she offered. She'd be disappointed if he changed his mind now, but she couldn't force him to share. Not when she had secrets she wasn't prepared to reveal yet.

"It was a lifetime ago. Feels like it happened to someone else." He scrubbed his free hand over the back of his neck. "I was just a kid."

"If it happened fifteen years ago, you *are* a different person. We all change and grow. I know *I'm* not the same person I was when I started college."

He flinched, and she knew he was thinking about what she'd gone through. His jaw clenched. But he started talking.

"I was headed for college, with a scholarship to UCLA in my grasp, when my world fell apart. My girlfriend, Camilla, informed me she was pregnant."

Lauren's hand clenched around his. Even though she'd expected to hear a child had been involved after Mamó's earlier comments, Lauren still took the news like a shot to the gut.

*Another woman had carried Ray's child.*

The knowledge made her raw. She couldn't squeeze a word past the constriction in her throat. She shouldn't care. Theirs was not a romantic connection. Being so cozy these last few days had given a false sense of intimacy. Nothing had changed.

Ray rubbed his thumb over her wrist. "We had one of those on again, off again relationships—mostly because she wanted constant attention and I was wrapped up in making movies. Neither of us was thinking long-term. At least I didn't think so. She knew I'd planned to go to Los Angeles whether I got the scholarship or not. The University of California Los Angeles is arguably the best school for film and television in the world."

"I remember reading an article stating that you won an award for a documentary on homeless runaways that had scholarship money attached to it."

"The Stahling Award. That's when I knew I had a good chance at going to UCLA. The award carries a lot of prestige. Along with my other awards and a short film, it was the complete package."

He hadn't been wrong. He'd gone to UCLA and become one of their biggest success stories. But something wasn't adding up. Something must have happened with the baby. Or maybe there hadn't been a baby at all?

"Was Camilla lying when she said she was pregnant?"

"No. Mamó would have known."

He got up and poured another glass of wine. He held the bottle up, silently asking if she wanted some. She shook her head. Sipping, he stared out the window.

"My world shattered. The last thing I wanted was a kid. But I'd been raised by my grandmother and my aunt—two widows, basically single mothers. I knew the hardships they'd faced. They raised me to take responsibility for my actions. I couldn't walk away from my kid and everything they'd taught me."

"You proposed?" she guessed, feeling for the young Ray who'd had all his dreams disrupted.

"I didn't love her. We'd only hooked up in our senior year. But the kid was mine, so, yeah, I proposed. Camilla and her mother started making rush wedding plans. She told me she wanted the ceremony right away, so she wouldn't be showing in her gown. I was committed. When didn't matter to me. Providing for my family did, so I started looking for a better job."

"You didn't consider taking Camilla with you to Los Angeles?"

"I considered it, but the scholarship was for dorm housing, so I'd have needed to work. And probably Camilla, too, which would be difficult with a newborn. At least in Queens we'd have family support nearby. But I wasn't giving up. I might have to do night courses, but I started putting in applications to New York film schools. Camilla had a fit when she realized."

"She thought she'd be going with you to Los Angeles?"

"Oh, yeah. She said if I could be a director she could be an actress. I laughed at her."

"Uh-oh." The word escaped without thought. Never a good idea to laugh at a woman—certainly not a pregnant one. The fact her aspirations had been somewhat misguided would only have made it worse.

"Not my shiniest moment," he confessed. "But my tolerance was stretched thin by then. I explained my reasoning. She didn't care—said I was jealous of her and insisted we go. I refused. Said I wasn't taking a child to California. She left in a huff."

Lauren closed her eyes, briefly shutting out his pain. She saw the train wreck coming. His stoic delivery as he relived the tragic memory was not fooling her for a moment. Aching for him, she stood and went to him. Wrapping her arms around his waist, she laid her head on his back and just held him. A fine tremor shook his body, revealing the hurt he tried to hide. He laid his hand over hers.

"I'm so sorry," she whispered.

"At that time we were only days away from the wedding. I should have figured out something was off when she stopped yammering at me over details I couldn't care less about. And she'd begun avoiding Mamó. I didn't notice. Hell, I couldn't even put a good face on it at that point. The less time I spent with her the better."

"Oh, Ray."

"I was at the church, dread heavy in my gut, and Mamó came into the little room where I was waiting. She knew how hard everything was for me."

"She never encouraged you to go?"

"No. She supported my decision to stay and raise my child. But she couldn't let me go through with the ceremony when she no longer sensed a child."

"What did you do?"

"I challenged Camilla. At first she refused to see me. Then she tried to deny it. But I knew. When I demanded someone go for a pregnancy test she broke down and claimed she'd lost the baby. She said she still loved me and now we could go to Los Angeles together. It made me sick to my stomach."

"She aborted the baby?"

"She denied it. Still does, as far as I know. But she was lying. She got pregnant to hook me and got rid of the baby when it threatened her plans."

The muscles in his back flexed as he braced his body to control the shaking. To disguise what Camilla's betrayal had done to him.

"You don't believe she ever intended having the baby."

The breath left his body and he unlinked her hands to turn and study her. He cupped her face, stared into her eyes. "How can you know that?"

"I'm beginning to know *you*. Camilla's perfidy was

painful, but having an innocent life trivialized made it worse."

"It wasn't just an innocent life. It was my child. Her treachery crushed me. Her total disregard for my child's life—that destroyed me." His jaw clenched as he fought for composure. "She stole seed from me and tossed a life away as if it meant nothing. All for a trip to Hollywood. How could I go to UCLA when I knew the lure of Hollywood was what had caused my child to lose his life?

"Ray..." Her heart broke for him.

"For about a week I punished myself. Pulled all my applications from the local schools, grabbed my camera, and hit the streets. I found destitution, despair, disassociation, defeat. These weren't the teenagers I had filmed before. They had been survivors. These people had given up entirely. After three days I couldn't stand it and I dragged myself home. Mamó was waiting for me. She embraced me, fed me, scolded me and shamed me. In the face of all I'd seen, her steadfast love humbled me. The next day she told me to get over the self-pity, pack my bags, and leave for Los Angeles, already. I'd seen what defeat did to a person. Damned if I was going to let Camilla steal my soul. So I followed Mamó's advice and never looked back."

"I'm glad you did. None of what happened was your fault."

"I made a child with her. I let her talk me into unprotected sex. *Stupid.* I was an eighteen-year-old boy, and she'd teased me past the point of control. But that's on me."

"The fact that you accept the responsibility makes you a good man. If you'd walked away unscathed you would be no better than her. But you cared. You mourned. You went on to be a brilliant film-maker. Truly, the world would be a sadder place if you had turned your back on Hollywood."

"Thank you." He pressed his forehead to hers. Tension drained from him. "Most of the time I can bury the memories. But being back has brought up a lot of those old emotions. It doesn't help that the gossip continues."

"Do you ever see Camilla?"

"No." A simple yet harsh statement. "I rarely come to the neighborhood."

"You shouldn't let the past keep you away. Mamó is so happy to have you at the house. A few stray comments amongst friends are nothing to some of the stuff I've seen in the tabloids. If you were around more the gossip would fade away from natural attrition—which would be good, because you're going to want to visit Mamó when you find a real fiancée."

Okay, that was too much. She stepped back. No doubt Camilla's escapades would dwindle when news of Ray's impending fatherhood got around.

Should Lauren tell him now?

No. It wasn't the right time. She didn't want him associating her news with the loss he had suffered in the past.

"I'm not interested in another fiancée."

An arm at her waist didn't let her go far. Long fingers traced the keyhole in her bodice. "Did I tell you how lovely you look tonight?"

"You did." And the desire in his eyes had repeated the message over and over throughout the night.

She'd wanted to make him notice her, and she had succeeded, all right. To the point it had almost backfired on her. The searing weight of his gaze had followed her all night, and her body had responded with heightened awareness until she could barely concentrate. There she had stood, rubbing elbows with the rich and powerful, and she'd struggled to put together coherent sentences. Fortunately the fact that a friend of the mayor's wife had heard of By Arrangement had caught her attention and grounded her in the conversation so she didn't actually embarrass herself.

The desire was back in his eyes now, burning brighter

than ever, making her nerves tingle and her body heat. She much preferred seeing passion over pain in his sea-blue eyes. And, oh, he smelled good.

She missed being held by him. So, with luxury surrounding her, New York lit up at her feet, and a hard man pulling her close, she surrendered her control.

Rising on her toes, she kissed the hard line of his jaw. "Are you just going to look? Or do you plan to do something about it?"

# CHAPTER TEN

RAY NEEDED NO further urging. He swept her into his arms and carried her to his room. Towards his bed. *Oh, yeah.* Satisfaction roared through him.

The thought of Lauren in his bed touched off something primitive in him.

Probably because it had taken so long to get her there. From the very beginning their sexual encounters had been steamy, exciting and clandestine. They were like flint and paper—sparking off each other until antagonism flashed to passion and they rushed to find the first private space available.

He'd never had better sex.

And it should have been enough.

He wasn't a possessive man when it came to women. Generally he preferred to keep things as unencumbered as possible, going to a hotel or to her place. He didn't trust easily. Women were a pleasure, not a commitment.

Rehashing his past had been like opening a vein: painful and potentially hazardous. What good could come of it? None, in his regard. He never talked about himself. Yet he'd felt compelled to share with Lauren. Bringing her to New York had probably been a mistake. Their closeness gave a false impression of intimacy.

Tonight he didn't care. He couldn't get too close.

Setting her on her feet, he sought out the side zipper

he'd spied during his frequent perusals of her throughout the night.

His hadn't been the only eyes on her during the reception. The attention she'd drawn had caused a low level animosity to burn under his skin.

She was *his*, damn it. Yet he'd also been proud to be with her. Smart, beautiful, poised—she was the total package.

He kissed her, hard and deep, then stepped back. "Take this off for me."

A shy smile greeted his request—unusual for the confident woman he knew her to be—but her delicate fingers went to the alluring blue straps that had tantalized him all night. Enchanted, he perched on the edge of the bed, prepared to enjoy her performance.

With a flick of her fingers the straps were loosened. A shimmy of her hips and the cobalt fabric pooled at her feet.

Sweet, merciful angels.

He sucked in a breath. It lodged in the back of his throat. She stood in nothing more than a black lace thong and mile-high shoes so sexy they made her pretty legs look like they reached clear to heaven.

Being in her arms was as close as he'd probably ever get.

"You should breathe," she advised him, her confidence fully restored.

She walked to him, all creamy skin and soft curves. Wedging herself between his spread knees, she started undoing buttons.

"Your turn."

"I've never seen anything more beautiful than you." He urged her down to him, kissed her lips, her chin, the side of her neck, working his way to luscious bounty.

She hugged his head to her and he felt her mouth against his hair. In that moment he felt cherished. She always brought intensity to their encounters. This was different—slower, softer.

*They* were different—no longer acquaintances scratching a passionate itch. She'd met his family, they'd traded secrets, slept together without making love; it was more than he'd had with anyone since leaving New York.

And it was more than he wanted to think about. Time to stop thinking and start touching.

Lying back, he took her with him and then rolled over so she lay beneath him, flushed and dewy-eyed.

"You're not usually so shy." She linked her arms around his neck and smiled at him. "This is going to be difficult to accomplish unless you remove these clothes."

"I don't want to stop touching you."

"Excellent argument. But it doesn't solve our problem."

"We have all night, Dynamite, a soft bed, and no need to rush. Short of being evacuated, I plan to make love to you all night long."

"All night? You *are* feeling frisky."

"I've spent the last few nights with this lovely little tush tucked up next to me. But because of your rules I couldn't do anything but hold you." He surged to his feet and stripped off his clothes. In less than a minute he'd joined her back in bed. "Until now. Frisky? Oh, yeah."

"So…oh…you're saying…uh…you cheated?"

Lauren arched under Ray's talented touch. He knew all her hot buttons and stroked them to maximum effect. True to his promise he took his time, building sensation on sensation, his touch in equal parts tender and demanding.

He smiled against her cheek. "Every chance I got."

He did something with his fingers that stole her ability to speak.

She tried to reciprocate, but all she could do was surrender to his erotic assault. She understood that he sought to escape the demons he'd revealed earlier. It had hurt to see him struggle through his vulnerability tonight, but no sign of it remained as he urged her with mouth, hands and body to mind-blowing responsiveness.

He bit her earlobe, nuzzled behind her ear, sending tingles sparking over heightened nerves. *Yesss.* She happily sacrificed her body to help him through the night.

Lauren lay with Ray curled around her and stared out the wide picture window into the predawn sky. Even at this height she saw lights in surrounding buildings, heard sirens and other city chatter. New York really never stopped.

And neither did her mind.

True to his word, Ray had pleasured her well into the night. Her body was boneless with satisfaction. And still Ray's story kept repeating in her head. What a tragic introduction to adulthood. How did someone *do* that to a person?

She rubbed her belly.

How did someone use another life with such capriciousness, such cruelty? It was unconscionable. And it made her question her own decision to withhold news of their child from Ray.

No doubt he'd be upset.

And he had every right to be.

She might be carrying the baby, but he or she was as much a part of Ray as Lauren. It shamed her to remember how easily she'd dismissed his interest in the child because she hadn't wanted to deal with her child's father. How arrogant of her to think he wouldn't want to be a part of his child's life simply because he had a demanding career and a high-profile lifestyle.

He said he loved kids, and the confidence and care with which he'd handled young Lulu proved his claim. Most men were afraid to hold a child that young. Not Ray. He had reached for her with genuine affection.

Suddenly she longed for the day he held their child.

The time to tell him had come.

In fact she worried that she should have told him last night, but she stood by her decision to wait—to give him distance from the misery he'd relived. She couldn't prevent the past from rising up when she told him he was going to be a father, but she could make sure he was in a better frame of mind.

Today they would tour the city. They'd be playing tourist, but Ray would also be working. She'd be careful to give him his space, to watch his mood. And when the time was right she'd share her precious news.

A helicopter! Lauren wavered between being thrilled and terrified. Dressed in jeans and a black sweater under the red leather jacket, she let Ray strap her into her seat. Once he'd settled in his own seat, and they both had headphones on, she reached for his hand.

"Don't let go," she implored him, not caring if the mayor's aide heard from his seat up-front.

"I won't." He brought her hand to his mouth and kissed her knuckles.

"What are you looking for today?"

"I'm doing a futuristic police procedural. The story is set fifty years in the future. I'll be looking at parts of the city with modern elements."

"Oh."

Well, *boo*. She'd hoped to see more than just architecture. So much for playing tourist. Still, it would be fun to see some of the other boroughs. And they were flying. Surely she'd catch a glimpse of something interesting.

"Can we at least fly by the Statue of Liberty?"

He squeezed her fingers. "We're starting with the statue. What would a film in New York be without a shot of the famous landmark? Don't worry. You'll see plenty of sights."

The helicopter lifted off, the world dropping away beneath her. Lauren clutched Ray's hand. They were leaving from the roof of their hotel, so they already had some elevation. For a moment the surrounding buildings seemed too close, but as the helicopter gained height they grew smaller.

Her breath caught. The panoramic view stunned her senses with the sheer vastness of the city. She waited for the vertigo, but it never came. The wristband the pilot had given her must be working.

"We have to land at Ellis Island." The mayor's aide, Felton Smith, a balding Asian American, addressed them through their headsets. "Helicopter landings are restricted at Liberty Island. A National Park representative will be there to greet us and take us over to the statue."

"National Park?" Lauren asked. "So it's not run by New York?"

"No," Felton confirmed. "Coolidge declared the statue a national monument in 1924, and in 1933 Franklin Roosevelt transferred jurisdiction to the National Park Services. You probably aren't going to want to film right on the island. Unless it's integral to the plot, the view is better from a distance."

Ray nodded. "We'll probably replicate the parts we need at the studio, but I like authenticity and it's been years since I've been to see the statue."

Within minutes the helicopter began to descend on Ellis Island. Having the earth rise to meet them got to Lauren, so she closed her eyes, taking comfort in Ray's hold on her hand. The bump of their landing was so skilled she barely felt it.

A park ranger in a crisp green uniform stepped forward to greet them. Ranger Paceco had graying brown hair and a military demeanor. After introductions, he gave a curt nod.

"Ms. Randall, Mr. Donovan—welcome to Ellis Island. How can I be of service today?"

Ray explained his mission as they walked toward a pier where several boats were moored.

Ranger Paceco stopped next to a speedboat. "Let's take you over. We'll give you the full tour."

Lauren looked longingly over her shoulder at the huge brick building housing so much American history. "Will we have time to take a peek inside when we come back?"

Ray wrapped an arm around her waist. "We'll see if we can find some time." He glanced significantly at the mayor's aide, who looked down at his tablet with a frown.

The speedboat made short work of the trip between islands. It seemed longer because of the cold. Lauren snuggled next to Ray on the bench seat, thankful for his body heat and the red leather coat.

From the shelter of his arm she watched the statue grow bigger and bigger, until she towered over their approach, a symbol of welcome and freedom. She was awe-inspiring. Lauren could only imagine how emotional it would have been to see her at the end of a cramped ocean voyage—the embodiment of a new beginning.

The manicured grounds were immaculate—a sign of the respect and pride the rangers took in their care of the lady. The stairs spiraling upward seemed never-ending. But, oh, the view was worth it.

The ranger gave them ten minutes to themselves. Ray whipped out his camera and started shooting, climbing right up to the glass.

No way was she leaning forward to look down. Her heart was already pumping out adrenaline. But she could still see the city in the distance. And New Jersey on the other side. Spectacular. She took a few pictures with her phone.

She admitted to being a homebody. She liked the comfort of having her things around her. Yet standing in a piece of history, with the world literally spread out before her, she acknowledged the appeal of traveling. Especially when you got VIP treatment.

Thinking of Ray, she sought him out. Her heart jumped into her throat when she saw him pressed right up against the glass, filming straight down.

"Ray." She took a step toward him, then stopped.

She wanted to leap across the space, wrap herself around his leg, and demand he come down from there. But the element of adventure was so much a part of him. She couldn't hold him back by placing her fears on him.

To ground herself she wrapped an arm around a newel post and eyed him anxiously.

"Just a minute more, Dynamite." His balance shifted as he bent even further forward.

*"Ohmigoodness."*

The man had a death wish. If he didn't fall to his death, she'd do it for him. She might anyway. And suddenly the world was spinning—not because he was falling, but because *she* was. Falling hard. For him.

She loved this crazy, thoughtful, manipulative, brilliant, stubborn, funny man.

Seeing him poised on the brink of a two-hundred-foot fall shot that knowledge home like nothing else. And—oh, goodness—the enormity of the emotion dwarfed all previous relationships. Including that dork in college. His name wouldn't even come to mind.

Ray filled her to the exclusion of everything else.

"Hey." Suddenly he stood in front of her, lifting her face to him. "I'm fine. With the glass, there's no chance of falling."

"Tell that to my racing heart." She wrapped her arms around herself.

"It's perfectly safe." He held his camera out to her. "And I got an incredible shot."

She didn't bother to look. "Oh, that's all right, then."

She pushed past him toward the stairs. He'd just become her whole world and he was doing things like testing the weight factor of the glass in the crown of the Statue of Liberty. He was going to get himself killed before he met his child.

*His child.* Oh, heavens. She had to tell him. To wait

another moment just seemed wrong. Except for the ever-vigilant Felton Smith and Ranger Paceco. You didn't tell the man you loved he was going to be a father in front of an audience.

"Hey, hey, hey." He caught up to her, swung her into his arms. "I'm sorry." He kissed her softly. "It's so amazing I got carried away." He tucked his camera in his backpack. "Here, come with me. Let me show you what I see."

He climbed up next to the glass and held out his hand.

She shook her head. "I don't think I can."

"I'll have you."

He caught the hand she'd instinctively raised to meet his and pulled her up next to him. Vertigo rose, but he wrapped both arms around her. His firmness and strength surrounded her.

"Okay?" he whispered in her ear.

She nodded, her body tense in his grasp. "Don't let go."

"I won't." Holding her close, he pointed. "That's Queens. And over there is Manhattan. See the spire? That's our hotel."

Cradled in his arms, she listened as he brought his world to life for her. Slowly she relaxed against him, enjoying his enthusiasm. He told her about his movie and she saw the wonder of his vision through his eyes.

Paceco finally signaled it was time to go.

Ray carefully helped her down. "Maybe it'll cheer you up to hear that Felton has made time to visit Ellis."

She blinked up at him. She always focused on his need for control, but the truth was he could also be incredibly giving. He was sacrificing part of his siting agenda to let her play tourist. And the timing would work out perfectly. When they got to Ellis Island she'd pull him aside. As soon as she had him alone she'd give him the news.

The ride back to Ellis Island seemed twice as long as the trip over. On the other hand she barely felt the cold, because she was trapped in her head.

Excitement and anxiety played tug-of-war with her emotions.

She didn't know what she wanted his reaction to be. Excitement, of course. But with his history she knew that was a lot to expect. She wanted him to be pleased, to start thinking of a future together.

Heavens, did she *want* a future together? Until yesterday she'd still been contemplating sole custody.

*Don't get ahead of yourself, girl,* her head warned her heart.

Finally the boat arrived at Ellis Island. As the group neared the building Lauren turned to their guides and upped the wattage of her smile. "Would it be okay for us to just wander around on our own for a few minutes?"

"Of course." Ranger Paceco offered his hand. "I'll leave you to your wanderings. If you need me, just have one of the rangers call me."

"You've been very helpful." Ray shook his hand. "I should have come over more when I was a kid."

"Sometimes we need age to appreciate things. Take care, now." He nodded and took his leave.

"I'll meet you at the chopper in forty minutes," Felton said. He already had his phone in his hand as he walked toward a bench.

"Nice move, Randall." Ray draped an arm around her shoulders. "I was beginning to feel crowded." He nuzzled his nose into her hair. "Mmm. You smell good." Moving toward the building, he asked her, "So, do you have family that came through Ellis Island?"

"My great-great-grandfather on my father's side. He was six when he came over from England in 1908."

"Cool. Mamó's grandmother came over from Ireland. Hey, I'm pretty sure that was 1908. Maybe they stood in line at the same time?"

"It's a romantic notion." She eyed his profile through her lashes. "And I can see a story brewing in that head of yours. This trip is getting to you. You don't usually do relationship movies."

"It's good to stretch yourself. What are you doing?" He stopped when she tried to direct him toward a bench in the sun. "The entrance is that way."

"I know. I need to talk to you."

At the bench her knees gave out and she gratefully sank down on the stone seat.

"I have something to tell you."

"Are you okay?" Dropping down next to her, he tucked a wisp of hair behind her ear. "You've gone pale."

"I'm fine." She gathered his hands in hers, hoped he wouldn't feel the tremors through her gloves, and looked at them rather than at him. This should be easier. Shouldn't it be easy to tell the father of her child?

"Lauren, what is it? You're shaking." He wrapped her hands in both of his and rubbed them to generate warmth.

"You'll be shaking in a moment."

"Now you're scaring me. Just tell me."

Deep breath…slow release. She looked into his concerned blue eyes. "I'm pregnant."

Shock knocked him back. A flash of joy, and then his expression closed down. His eyes narrowed and he looked out over the water.

"A baby."

His flat tone revealed nothing.

"That explains your upset stomach. And your refusal of wine and coffee. How long have you known?"

"S-Since the wedding." Hating the shake in her voice, she cleared her throat, tried for more confidence. "I did an early pregnancy test that morning. I would have confirmed it with my doctor this week, except I've been here."

He stood, thrust his hands in his pockets. "So you've known for four days and you haven't said anything?"

He made it sound unreasonable. "It was unexpected. I needed time to think."

Anguish flashed across his face.

"No!" Her heart constricted in a punishing vice, she jumped to her feet, rushed to him, placed a reassuring hand on him arm. "Not about aborting the child. I'd *never* make that choice."

"Then what was there to think about?" he demanded. "What was more important than telling me I'm going to be a father?" He pinned her with a hard gaze. "I'm supposing I *am* the father?"

*Wow.* She retreated a step, then two.

"Yes, of course." Offended, she fisted her hands at her sides. "Are you questioning your paternity?"

"I remember the broken condom." He turned away, ran a shaking hand through thick hair. "Though my attorney will want a paternity test. I can't believe this. I must have super-swimmers. You should have told me, Lauren. All week we've been together. On the plane, at Mamó's." He scrubbed his face. "Hell, last night I poured my heart out to you about the child I lost."

"Right—and I was supposed to break into the middle of that story with *By the way I'm pregnant*?" She wrapped her arms around herself, trying to hold herself together as his words tore her apart. "It wasn't the time. This week hasn't been the time. You've been worried about your grandmother, dealing with the whole fake engagement thing, as well as this siting business. I didn't even know about the trauma of confronting your past."

*This was a mistake*, she thought. *I should have waited.*

The backs of her knees hit the stone bench again. She sank down. She'd known after his revelation last night that he'd have a hard time with her news. She hadn't expected him to be thrilled, but after their time together here in New York she hadn't expected him to be hurtful either.

He came to stand over her. "If you're expecting a proposal, think again. I'm not eighteen anymore."

"I'm not expecting anything from you." A slide to the

left gained her some breathing room. "I'm a successful, professional woman. Don't worry. I can take care of myself and my child."

"*Your* child." He dropped down next to her, but half turned away. "I get it now. You weren't going to tell me."

"Don't be so dramatic. Hollywood is too small to hide a pregnancy. Of course I was going to tell you."

"When?"

"Why do you care?"

"What?" He pinned her with an astounded stare over his shoulder.

"You've made it clear you're not interested in the baby." No need to cast a feature film to get that point across. "Fine with me. Consider yourself uninvited to the party."

"Seriously? You're going to pout because I didn't get down on one knee?"

"No, I'm going to live my life around my child. I'm not a self-important prima donna, too worried about protecting myself to know if I'm happy about being a parent or not."

She needed to get away from him. *Now.*

On her feet, she faced him. "Keep your ring. I never wanted it anyway." She hiked her chin toward the helicopter. "You should go on with your tour. I'm going to hang out here for a couple of hours."

Gaze locked on the entrance to the huge brick building, she put one foot in front of the other. She just needed to get inside before she broke down. No way was she giving him the satisfaction of seeing her cry.

After a few steps he grabbed her arm. "I'm not leaving you here alone."

"You don't have a choice," she informed him. "I'm all grown up, Ray. I can make my own decisions and get myself home." She glared pointedly at his hand on her arm.

He released her. "Why?"

"Because you're not responsible for me."

"No, why did you tell me now when you had no plan to do so?"

"You scared me." Giving him half the truth, she waved toward the statue towering in the distance. "I thought you should know you had a kid before you did something fool-hardy and died."

"Listen, come with me." His hand dropped away. "I'm not handling this well, and I'm sorry. I need time to process everything."

"And we both know you'll process better without me. I'll see you back at Mamó's.

"Okay." He gave a gruff nod. "I'll arrange for a car to pick you up at Battery Park. I'll text you with the information. They'll take you wherever you want to go."

*Home.* Could the driver take her to Hollywood?

It was where she longed to be—curled up on her couch with her grandma's quilt tucked around her, surrounded by familiar things, with her sister next door and her mother on the other end of the phone.

The fantasy burst, an impossible dream.

"Thanks," she said, for once happy with his need to ma-nipulate every situation. Then she continued toward the entrance, not wanting to watch him walk away.

She needn't have worried. She barely saw the doors through the tears blurring her vision.

# CHAPTER ELEVEN

Staying over in the suite tonight.

LAUREN STARED AT the text, numb both inside and out. Apparently she was supposed to process the fact she was pregnant immediately and then go on to share the news with him, but he needed most of the day and the night, too.

"Ray isn't coming home, is he?" Mamó set a tray on the coffee table and settled into her chair next to the couch, where Lauren sat trying to reproduce the image of home she'd created earlier.

"No. Business is keeping him in the city, so he's going to stay at the hotel again."

"You don't have to cover for him, dear." Mamó leaned forward to pour steaming liquid into a sturdy mug. "I made hot cocoa." Heaping spoons full of whipped cream followed. "I thought you could use the pick-me-up."

It was just the thing. "Thank you." Lauren accepted the mug, drank a small sip. The heat and the chocolate sent warmth and comfort rolling through her. "Mmm. Perfect."

"You told him, didn't you?"

"Mmm," Lauren hummed. She had too much pride to bad-mouth the woman's grandson in her own home. "He's processing."

"He didn't take it well." It wasn't a question.

"Let's say he was shocked." The truth, and yet far short of everything.

Mamó nodded. "Which translates to being a jerk."

"I'll stick with shocked." Lauren sighed. "Now I've calmed down I recognize I was a tad hormonal and perhaps overly sensitive."

"All the more reason for him to take care of you." Sadness tugged at the corners of Mamó's eyes and her lips trembled as she sipped from her cup. "He's never cared much for surprises. I blame losing his parents at such a young age."

Lauren remembered the shock and horror of losing her high school friend to suicide in their senior year. It had consumed her whole world for months. How much worse would it be to lose family? To lose both parents at the same time?

"I don't even want to imagine the pain he must have experienced. And then Camilla pulled her heartless stunt. It's understandable he dislikes surprises."

Unfortunately she knew of no other way to deliver news of a baby. Especially an unplanned pregnancy.

"He told you about Camilla?" Surprise chased despair from Mamó's face. "He's never told anyone, as far as I know. Not even Ellie. I had to piece parts of it together myself."

"It's not a pretty story."

"Far from it. I was so proud of him. I knew how much he wanted to go to UCLA, how hard he'd worked for the Stahling Award. But he set aside his future in Hollywood for a future with his family. It was the smart thing, the responsible thing to do. It shattered him when he realized Camilla had murdered his child to mortgage her own career."

"Murdered...?" Lauren murmured. He hadn't used the word last night, but it sounded like Ray. It was very telling.

"His word." Mamó unknowingly confirmed it. "Most men would have been happy to get out of a forced marriage. Ray was committed from the beginning. I know my boy. I read all those tabloids where they call him a confirmed bachelor, and say how he prizes his privacy. They've got him all wrong. The truth is he has a big heart. He's just learned to guard it carefully."

"He's afraid of being hurt again." Lauren related to that sentiment. Better to be alone than to give up a part of your soul.

"You're different."

That caught Lauren's attention. "What do you mean?"

"The way he is with you. It's different from when he's with other women. He doesn't just look at you—he watches you as if he can't look away."

"Really?" She cringed a little at the hope in her voice.

"This isn't an easy time for either of you. I implore you to give him a chance. Your little ones deserve to have both parents in their lives."

"Lives?" Lauren croaked.

"Yes, dear. You're having twins."

Mamó says twins.

Ray read Lauren's text over and over. Twins. *Hell.* This was news he could have waited to hear. He couldn't stop thinking, wondering, worrying. Any minute now his head would implode.

When he couldn't take another second he went on the move. He rented a car, took the 87 in the Bronx and headed north. Blowing by Albany, he chased the Catskills, his mood black.

He took a curve, low and tight, and came out on a straightway. Punching the accelerator, he raced through the night, going faster than he should in an act Lauren would no doubt consider foolhardy.

His foot lowered, squeezing out a little more speed.

He was an adult. The last thing he needed was a woman telling him how to act.

The rental handled well, but his plan to go for a drive

in order to get away from his thoughts wasn't working out. Okay, it was a flawed plan. Where his head went, his thoughts followed. And, no matter how hard he tried to focus on something else, his mind kept wrapping back to Lauren and the babies she carried.

He tried thinking about his upcoming film and the sites he'd seen today, but honestly he didn't remember much after the bomb she'd dropped.

Mamó's condition couldn't even hold his attention. And the industry awards scheduled a few days away barely blipped on his radar—which peeved him, because he really wanted to sweep the season and this was the biggie. Not since his first film had he hit the trifecta of awards. To do so again would prove he had staying power.

Was it just yesterday he'd asked Lauren to go with him? This week stretched out forever in his head.

He ground his teeth, mad at the world, mad at himself, mad at Lauren, mad at life.

Mad at the world because, seriously, why him? The first time had completely undone him. He might not survive a second time.

Mad at himself because of the way he'd managed to muck things up. He wasn't handling it well, but he couldn't get a grip.

Mad at Lauren because she was the one doing this to him. No matter how cockeyed that thinking was. Which only added guilt to the mix as well. *Hello.*

Mad at life for the whole mix.

And now twins.

It only made the situation worse to hear the news here in New York, after spending half a week mired in memories he'd spent fifteen years burying skull-deep.

He slowed for another curve, flinched as headlights hit him in the eyes. It was the first traffic he'd encountered in a while—not surprising, considering the late hour on a work night. Soon he'd have to think about turning around and heading back to the hotel.

It might be a cop-out, but no way could he face cuddling up in his old bedroom with Lauren. At the same time he'd miss having her in his bed. It didn't make sense, yet it was one of the loops his head kept tracking.

That and memories of that horrific summer. He'd been shocked and devastated when Camilla had broken the news. He'd tried to hold it together, but in the end he'd bolted.

It had crushed his spirit to give up on UCLA, but he'd seen no other choice. The kid had to come first. How idealistic he'd been. But even in retrospect he couldn't see playing his hand any differently.

Except to wear a damn condom.

Resentment festered. Why did this keep happening to him?

He felt victimized, and yet there was no fault here. They'd had protected sex. Hell, *he'd* been the one to provide the condom that broke.

Fighting off weariness, he rolled his neck, stretching muscles, working out kinks. He owed Lauren a better apology. More, he owed her his support. She was just as much a victim as him. Yet deep down he couldn't help feeling as if she'd done this to him.

Because she'd kept the news from him.

He'd deserved to know as soon as she knew. The babies might be in her body, but they were as much a part of him as they were of her. He had *rights*, damn it. Being the last one to know, having no say in decisions, didn't sit well with him. How could he protect his children when he didn't know what was going on?

Anger lashed at his nerves.

Back to being mad at himself, because he couldn't stop being upset with Lauren. She might have been blameless in the conception, but she had withheld the news, taken the power of knowledge from him. Tried to push him away. Still was, come to that. Who knew how long she would have taken to tell him if Mamó's depression hadn't pushed them together?

Well, Lauren needed to adjust her thinking. He might be a perpetual bachelor, but he was damned if he'd be a sperm donor. If he'd fathered a baby—babies!—he'd be a part of his children's lives.

And, no, he didn't doubt the babies were his.

He knew Lauren—knew her integrity and the value of family to her. Never in a million years would she play false with the paternity of her child.

And she'd never hurt her child. *Children.* He believed that completely.

Yet he took little comfort in the thought.

Never would he have contemplated it of Camilla either. He couldn't conceive of it himself, so he had a hard time putting the unconscionable act in anyone's head. Then again, for Camilla the baby had been a means to an end—a tool to get what she wanted, never meant to see life.

And he had to put that aside.

The past had no bearing on the current situation. He needed to get past it and move on.

Desperate for a break, he took the next exit and pulled into the parking lot of an all-night diner. The waitress gave him a choice of the many empty booths. He slid into one next to the window, a distance away from the other two occupied tables.

"Coffee, please."

"Anything else?" the waitress asked. Young, slightly plump, with a high ponytail and pretty features, she waited patiently for his response. Her name tag read "April."

Had he eaten? He scrubbed his hands over his face, barely able to string two thoughts together. Whatever. He had no appetite.

"That's all, thanks."

She nodded and wandered away.

Ray turned his gaze to the window and got smacked with his own reflection. He looked haggard, but otherwise the same as he had this morning. That was just *wrong*. His life had changed; surely his appearance should show it?

April returned. She set down a big mug of steaming coffee and slid a plate with a large slice of chocolate cream pie in front of him.

He looked up at her. "I didn't order this."

"I know, but we're known for our chocolate cream pie. And you look a mite troubled. Pie always helps me when I'm troubled."

Looking at the whipped cream piled high, he felt his appetite come rushing back. He tipped his chin up. "Thanks."

"You want to talk about it?"

He tasted the coffee, hummed his approval as he shook his head. "Anything but."

"Okay, then." She leaned against the facing booth. "You're that director guy, aren't you?"

"I've made a few movies," he acknowledged. Usually he'd politely shut her down, but she'd brought him pie and he welcomed the distraction. "Are you interested in movies?"

"I like a good flick, but my passion is fashion design."

He recalled his trip to Eve's and seeing Lauren's transformation. *Passion* summed it up. "Well, April, that's a fine profession."

A huge smile lit up her face. "Let me know if that family gets too loud." She winked. "I'll bring you another piece of pie."

She wandered off and he glanced at the family: a mother, father, and three kids somewhere between the ages of five and eight. They chattered and laughed as they ate. The oldest, a boy, was telling the story of some ride where he'd been scared but his dad had been there so he'd felt brave and lifted his arms and felt like he was flying.

"And then *I* got scared," the dad said. "Because I thought you were going to fly away."

At that point the mom sent the kids off to the bathroom. Once they'd trooped off, she murmured something to the dad and they shared a laugh and a kiss.

Their unity got to Ray. Their love and camaraderie at the end of a long day. It shouted family with a capital F. And he realized he wanted that—the love, the togetherness.

April brought him a full to-go cup along with his bill. He left her a hefty tip. Time to head back. Running only worked so long before you had to step up and face what you were running from.

"Mamó." Lauren's voice shook. "I'm bleeding."

"Oh, my dear." Mamó came from the kitchen to take Lauren's hands and lead her to the couch. Sitting next to Lauren, she held her hands over her belly. "May I?"

Lauren nodded.

Mamó laid her hands on Lauren's belly and concentrated. Heart tripping wildly, Lauren waited breathlessly.

"I sense no distress," Mamó announced, and Lauren allowed herself to breathe. "Is it heavy bleeding?" Mamó asked. "Are you in pain?"

"Spotting, mostly. No pain. But it's not good, is it?" Lauren squeezed the words through a sand-crusted throat. She wished she'd been to the doctor, had some indication of what this might mean. "I've always heard bleeding is bad when you're pregnant."

"Some things are natural. But much has been learned since I had my babies. You will feel better if you see a doctor."

Lauren squeezed Mamó's hands. "I will, yes."

"Then we will go. You have been through much these last few days. I'm so sorry for my part in causing you distress."

"Mamó—"

"No." The older woman shook her head, swiped at a tear. "Ray was right. It is not okay. I've worked myself into a state, wanting great-grandbabies, but it's not fair of me to pin my happiness on Ray's life. Seeing the problems I've caused, I realize it's not healthy for either of us." She patted Lauren's fingers. "You stay here. I'll get Ellie and your purse and we'll be on our way." She bustled off.

Lauren wrapped her arms around her babies and sat perfectly still. If she didn't move, nothing could happen to them. Where was Ray? She longed for his strength and support—could really do with some of his take-charge attitude right about now.

Mamó returned with Ellie and her purse and jacket. Ellie was dragging Lauren's luggage.

"Hey, I'm thinking positive. In case you're good to travel you'll have to leave from the hospital."

*Oh, right.* Lauren had made a flight reservation after her assistant had called with an emergency. Lauren had handled it, but she'd decided she needed to go home. Ray didn't want her here and she was needed in California. It was after she'd finished packing that she'd noticed the spotting.

She'd hoped to see Ray before she left, but she really couldn't think about all that right now. She was too worried about the twins to focus on anything else.

Mamó and Ellie bundled her up. And they were off. Lauren tagged Ray with a text. Yes, it was cowardly, but she didn't feel like fielding a lot of questions she didn't have answers for.

And he should *be* here, damn it.

Suddenly chilled, she shivered. All night she'd lain awake, wondering what his "processing" might result in. Would their children—oh, goodness, she still reeled at the reality of twins—would their twins bring them closer or drive them apart?

Perhaps that was her answer. Never had she felt so alone

as she had sleeping by herself in his bed last night. Not that she'd slept much.

She should be more understanding. Recalling her own shock and her struggle to adjust to the life-altering news, she should have a clue what he was going through. And she did. But it didn't stop her from resenting his continued silence.

It might be unfair of her to think so, but there was a difference in being uncommunicative when the other party existed in blissful ignorance than when they waited in breathless anxiety. He'd been the one to pull back. The way she saw it, he needed to be the one to come to her.

Now would be good. She really needed him.

I'm bleeding. Mamó is taking me to the hospital.

Fear punched into Ray's gut as he read Lauren's text. He immediately tried her phone, but she didn't answer. *Damn it.*

He dialed his grandmother. She answered on the first ring.

"Mamó, how is she?"

"I don't get any sense of distress from the babies. And I believe I would if they were in true danger. But to be safe we're taking Lauren to Emergency."

"Let me talk to her." Muffled voices rumbled on the other end of the line.

"She doesn't want to talk to you."

*Damn it.* Add anger to the fear and dread forming a ball in his chest. His fault. He shouldn't have put her off with texts last night and this morning.

"Put her on."

"She's not shutting you out," Mamó assured him. "She doesn't want to talk because she doesn't have any answers. She's holding it together, but she's scared. It doesn't help that she's out of her element here in New York."

"Ask her what I can do."

This time he heard Lauren answer clearly. "Just tell him to get here."

"She said—"

"I heard," he cut in. "Text me the address. I'm on my way."

Ray explained the situation to the major's aide, thanked him for his assistance, and hopped in the car waiting for him. He gave the driver the address and instructions to hurry. As the car raced toward Queens he kept his mind off worrying about Lauren and the babies by looking ahead.

He'd need to get Fred and Ethel to baby-proof the house and grounds. Maybe they'd have a recommendation for a nanny. Or perhaps Lauren knew someone.

No doubt she'd want to be a hands-on mom, but he wanted someone available to help so she didn't get worn out. It was a given she'd continue to work.

Calculating dates, he figured Lauren would be due in seven months, give or take a week or so, which put him a month into filming here in New York. Maybe he should chuck the location shots?

His shoulders tensed at the notion. There was an authenticity that came with location filming that couldn't be captured on a back lot or in a substitute spot. He'd figure something out.

Because he wasn't missing the birth of his children.

And this—whatever it ended up being—was just a blip. Mamó would have sensed it if something were wrong. Battling another surge of fear, he clung to the fact she hadn't felt any fetal distress. Everything would be all right.

The car hit the bridge, and he made a proclamation and a prayer. He had to believe.

The alternative just wasn't acceptable.

The driver changed lanes, cutting off a delivery truck with inches to spare. Ray gritted his teeth and held on. They couldn't move fast enough for him. He hated not knowing. Hated not being there for Lauren. How he longed to have her safe in his arms right now.

Again, his fault. He'd been punishing her for...what? Thinking of herself first? Adjusting to the fact she was going to be a mother? Letting him deal with his grandmother and his past before learning he was going to be a father?

What a hero he was.

Finally he spotted his destination. The driver pulled right up in front of the emergency room at Queens Hospital and Ray hopped out. He spoke briefly with Mamó and Ellie, then waved down a nurse. He recognized the woman from the neighborhood, and for once he was happy for the connection as she personally escorted him to the cubicle where Lauren was being treated.

"How is she?" he asked, his heart running a marathon in his chest.

"The doctor has seen Lauren and she's fine. The bleeding was due to some natural adjustments of the uterus. Nothing to worry about. But to be on the safe side he ordered an ultrasound. The technician is in with Lauren now."

"Thanks." Relief left him breathless.

"No problem." Arriving at a cubicle, she pushed the curtain aside. "Mr. Donovan," she announced. She patted him on the arm, said, "Congratulations, Daddy," and left.

"Ray." Lauren gave a glad cry of relief and reached for his hand.

He stepped forward, wrapped her fingers in his. "The nurse said you were fine."

She lay on a gurney while the technician ran a scope over her belly and monitored the machine next to her.

"That's what they tell me. More important, the babies are fine. Look."

First he leaned down and kissed her on the top of her head, disguising his huge relief. Seeing her animation,

touching her, reassured him more than any medical niceties could.

He glanced at the picture she indicated on the screen
but failed to make out anything until the technician directed his attention to two little heads and two sets of feet,
showed him the two beating hearts.

He slowly sank down on the side of the gurney next to
Lauren, overcome by this visual evidence of his children.
The twins were no more than a couple of inches big, but
they packed a big wallop.

The picture blipped as Lauren scooted over, making
more room for him. "Pretty awesome, huh?"

"Yes." The word *terrifying* came to mind. "I want to
be involved."

It was a bald statement.

Her gaze flew to the technician. "We don't need to talk
about that now."

For once he didn't care who heard his business. He'd
never been more certain of anything in his life. "I've been
an ass. I'm sorry."

"Stop." Lauren tightened her grip on his hand.

"I'll just check with the doctor." The technician handed
her a couple of tissues for the gel on her tummy and made
a discreet exit.

Ray took the tissues and wiped her clean, his touch
warm after the chill of the gel. "Lauren—"

"No." She laid a finger on his lips. "Before you go on I
need to say something."

Needing to feel more in control, she tugged her sweater
down and sat up.

"Yes, I thought you were being a jerk, but I was wrong.
And so were you. This is huge." She waved at the blank
screen that had so recently held images of their children.
"We're going to be parents. It's important, and it's not
something to rush. I already made that mistake. And I'm
sorry."

"I shouldn't have yelled at you."

"You were in shock. So was I. We need time, both of us, to come to grips with this change in our lives. And I mean more than a few hours—possibly more than a few days. And that's okay, because we have another seven months to figure everything out."

He lifted a sandy brow. "Ms. Clipboard? You're not going to be able to wait seven months for anything."

The corner of her mouth kicked up at that. "Probably not. But I know I want to do this right. And rushing isn't the way to do that."

"No rushing around for you, young lady," the doctor said, entering the cubicle. "You're carrying precious cargo."

He introduced himself to Ray.

"How are the twins, Doctor?" Ray asked. "Anything we should be concerned about?"

"Everything looks normal." The doctor included Lauren in his answer. "You'll want to see your doctor when you get home. In the meantime try to keep stress to a minimum—which means no rushing. But you're healthy...the babies are healthy. I see no reason why you can't fly."

"Thank you, Doctor." His assurances finally allowed her to relax.

"Congratulations to the both of you." He shook Ray's hand and departed.

"Well, that was good to hear." Ray helped her up. "Now, let's get you home."

"Listen, I'm not going back to Mamó's." She stood and looped the strap of her purse over her shoulder. "Something came up at work so I booked a flight earlier. I can still make it, so I'm going to go. It's for the best. It'll give both of us the extra space we need." She kissed his cheek.

"Wait, you can't go." He followed her out into the hall, pulled her to a stop. "We're just starting to actually communicate."

"We'll communicate better in Hollywood, when we're both back in the real world."

"You can't leave. You just got out of Emergency.

"And the doctor said I'm okay to fly."

"Come on, Lauren," he implored her. "It's not like you to pout."

"I don't pout."

Moving around him, she moved toward the lobby, where Mamó and Ellie waited. His arguments made her more determined to leave. She pulled her phone out and texted the cab company she'd called while waiting for the technician.

"What would you call running away? I thought you were done playing games?"

Serene mood shattered, she swung on him. "This isn't playtime for me, Ray. I'm not a paper doll. I've been there, done that, didn't like it. I won't apologize for making my own decisions." Not wanting to go there, she dropped her head on his chest, leaned on his strength. "You need to finish your visit with your grandmother, and I just want to go home."

His arms came around her, his hand fisting in her hair. "I don't need more time, Lauren. This scare has confirmed my feelings. I want to be a part of my children's lives. I'll let you go now. But factor me into your thinking—because I'm not going away."

# CHAPTER TWELVE

RAY STOOD IN THE middle of his room, surrounded by emptiness. All evidence of Lauren's presence was gone. Only her scent lingered. Honeysuckle and soap. He stared at the too-small bed where even she had defied the rules she'd set down, curling so sweetly into his arms.

He didn't spend the night with women. And he didn't bring them home. Those two steps prevented any misguided sense of intimacy from developing between him and his companions. Those two decrees were the bedrock of his rigidly practiced relationship controls, followed by:

*Never let sex control a decision.*
*Never get personal.*
*Never have unprotected sex.*

Those few restrictions had helped him live an uncomplicated life for the last fifteen years. Yet from the very beginning Lauren had slipped past his shields. She'd blown through the first two in one night.

You couldn't get any more personal than having family over for Thanksgiving. He should never have invited them…her…not even to drag Garrett out of his funk. But, hey, he'd figured he had his attraction for her under control. Heck, she'd irritated him as much as she'd turned him on—if not more. And her family on the premises should have guaranteed nothing was going to happen.

Best sex he'd ever had.

It hadn't mattered that they'd been in the laundry room, or that her parents had been down the hall. One smart remark too many had sparked the flame of passion, incinerating the barrier of restraint, creating an urgency not to be denied.

He'd only meant to quiet her with his mouth.

The taste of her had ignited his blood.

It was the last coherent thought he'd had until, heart racing, he'd collapsed against her and let the washing machine absorb his weight.

At the end of the night he'd shaken it off. Okay, it had happened. Lesson learned. He'd keep his distance in the future.

*Right.*

It should have helped that she was having the same discussion with herself.

It hadn't.

Twice more they'd hooked up. The urgency just as strong. The sex just as good. The broken condom should have been deterrent enough to prevent a third session—but, no. He'd just been glad he'd had condoms on him when the mood had struck, because the passion was so overwhelming he couldn't claim he would have stopped.

Add sleeping with her to his list of violations. He'd taken just as much satisfaction in holding her as she slept as he'd taken in pleasuring her lovely body. The last rule broken. The contentment he'd felt waking with her in his arms had overridden any thought of self-preservation.

He'd always been a rule-breaker, but not about this. The way he'd blown through his own rules should have warned him against asking her to accompany him to New York. Arrogance again. He'd missed her, so he'd thought he could give Mamó what she asked for while seducing Lauren into a vacation fling. A win-win for him.

And now they were to be parents.

He yanked his bag out of the closet and started emptying the drawers into it. With Lauren gone he felt a need to follow her to Hollywood. He stopped packing to text his friend's pilot and got an immediate response that the plane would be prepped and ready within two hours. His flight set, he tossed in his remaining items and zipped the bag.

To the pit of his soul he detested the need to alter his life for another unexpected pregnancy. Yet the one clear thing he'd taken away from the last two days was the desire to be a part of his children's lives.

The juxtaposition twisted him up inside. Deep down he knew he had to get past the resentment or he'd poison any relationship he established with Lauren and his kids.

Still he lingered, his thoughts in turmoil.

He dropped down on the bed, dragged Lauren's pillow from under the covers and buried his nose in the softness. The heady honeysuckle scent went to his head. Through all the uncertainty the one thing he did know was she'd touched him in ways no one else ever had.

"Ray." Mamó appeared in the bedroom doorway a little winded from her trip up the stairs. She carried something red clutched under her arm.

"Mamó." He hopped up and led her to the bed to sit.

She patted the bed beside her and he sat too.

"I'm sorry Lauren felt the need to leave early. Such a nice girl. I'm so glad you brought her with you."

"Yeah, it turned out to be more of a trip than I expected."

"I apologized to her and now I'll apologize to you. I'm sorry for my meddling, for letting my emotions get the better of me, for causing you so many problems."

"You may have caused a few complications. I managed the problems all on my own." There was a fine truth. In the scheme of things Mamó's preemptive engagement announcement had turned out to be a minor development. Hard to trump twins.

"I guess I don't have to tell you my news."

"Dear boy, I won't deny I'm pleased." She patted his knee. "I do regret my gift has been such a trial for you. To this day I mourn the part I played in ending your wedding."

"Don't." He draped an arm around her shoulders, took comfort in the strength of her thin frame. She was tougher than she looked. "None of what happened was your fault. I'm glad I learned the truth. If not for you, I would have married a woman I didn't love under false circumstances. The marriage would have ended anyway, because the child was the only reason I was with her."

"And will you propose to Lauren?"

A denial sprang to mind, yet he hesitated. "Truthfully, Mamó, I don't know how I feel. It's hard to unwrap the events of today from the events of the past."

"It shouldn't be. You were a boy then, just starting out. You're a man now, well established and successful in your field. Your feelings for Camilla were mild at best, your decisions based on honor and expedience. And she was using you. Your feelings for Lauren are deeper, stronger. She's successful in her own right. She's with you because she chooses to be, not because she needs you. You'll be partners in whatever manner you elect to go forward."

She made it sound so simple. But she didn't know the whole truth.

"Lauren came to New York as a favor to me." He explained the circumstances. "So, you see, we aren't actually romantically connected."

"Hmm. I think you're wrong. And you just proved my point. There was no need for her to help you. You may feel like you're caught in the same situation, but these women couldn't be more different. My advice is to stay focused on the present. Don't let the past cause you any more misery than it already has. Here."

She held out the red item she'd been carrying and as it unfolded he saw it was the coat he'd given Lauren. The one she'd refused. The one she'd looked so beautiful in when the weather had trumped her stubbornness.

His jaw clenched as he took it. Obstinate woman. He started to hand it back, to demand Mamó donate it to charity as he'd threatened Lauren he would. But he couldn't. He hated the thought of another woman wearing the coat.

A honk from the street announced the arrival of his taxi.

"There's your ride. Give me a hug." She wrapped him in her arms and for a moment he felt like he was ten years old again and she was his whole world.

He kissed her cheek. "You take care of yourself."

"I'll be good." She patted his cheek. "No more feeling sorry for myself. Besides, I have great-grandchildren to look forward to."

Well, *there* was an upside to the situation.

He helped her down the stairs, and then he was out the door and on the road.

A short while later he boarded the plane. He tossed his backpack and the red jacket into a seat and dropped down in the leather chair beside it. Soon they were in the air. The six-hour flight stretched ahead of him.

Leaning forward he stabbed his hands into his hair. Heck, he couldn't stand to spend any more time with himself. If he didn't find something besides his life to think about, he'd go insane.

"Good afternoon, sir." The flight attendant appeared. "Would you care for refreshments?"

Ray shook his head. "No thank you, Julie."

"May I secure these items?" She gestured to the backpack and jacket in the seat next to him.

"Leave them. That will be all for now."

The woman disappeared and Ray reached for his bag, drew out his camera and laptop. He'd organize his photos and video shots. That should occupy him for a while.

To start he sorted the work into three categories: family

and Mamó's birthday, the siting trip, and others. He soon noticed a commonality in all three. Lauren.

*Grr...* The point of this was to get away from thoughts of her. He began dropping all the photos of her into a separate file. It didn't take long to discover the problem with that plan. He lost nearly all his photos. Easily two-thirds of his pictures went into the "Lauren" file.

She'd obviously been a primary target for his lens.

Curious about what had drawn him, he went back and started looking from the beginning.

There were shots of her sleeping on the plane, pale and exhausted. He should have had a clue something was off right then. He called her Dynamite for a reason—because he never saw her going less than full out. She'd given him some excuse and he'd bought it, chalking her frailness up to pulling off her sister's big wedding, right during awards season, which would knock out any normal person.

Then came shots of her at the welcome party, surrounded by strangers, yet smiling and poised, all while under the duress of supporting a fake engagement. She really had been a good sport.

He grinned at the less than patient expression on her face in his bedroom as she tried to lay down her new rules. As if they could sleep in any sized bed without touching. He'd taken great delight in letting her break *that* rule.

Lauren at Mamó's party, looking elegant and feminine. He wanted to delete the picture of her with the hired dancer. But he left it as penance for the one of her with her head bent, hurt and sadness evident on her face and in her posture. His fault for insulting her matchmaking talents.

Not his best moment.

To make up for it he'd tried to tell Mamó he knew about her admirer before he left. She'd twittered and waved him off, saying she knew all about George's hot crush. And that someday she might do something about it.

Appalled all over again, he'd turned, looking for Lauren, and immediately realized his mistake.

Damn, he missed her.

Seeing her coat next to him, he curled his hand into a fist on the leather. Then he forced his fingers to loosen the fabric. He'd already sniffed her pillow today, like some lovesick pup. Besides, he could smell the honeysuckle from where he sat.

He wished she were here.

More shots of Lauren—in the hardware store, coming out of the spa, on the streets of New York, at the mayor's reception, stunning in that blue dress, flying over the city, on the boat to Liberty Island, in the crown… He'd even caught one of her when she'd wrapped herself around that newel post.

The fear on her face was stark. Real. Telling.

He looked into her eyes and adrenaline shot through his body as if he was prepared to defend, to protect, to battle—whatever it took to remove the anguish staring out at him.

Problem was he'd be fighting himself.

Lauren cared about him. It showed in every smile, in every indulgent look, in every censuring grimace—and she'd nailed him a few times—in every sultry glance.

His gaze landed on the one boudoir shot. He grinned, remembering he'd snapped it before she'd realized he held the camera.

She'd beat him back to bed after a steamy shower and sprawled half under the sheet, half on top, so the camera had caught the naked length of her back. Her blond hair was a messy knot on the top of her head, damp tendrils clung to her face and neck, and she looked directly into the camera, anticipating his return.

His blood heated and—

His breath caught.

He leaned forward. Blew up the shot. And stared right

into sleepy eyes, molten gold and shimmering with soft emotion.

*Love.*

He'd missed it at the time—damn camera—but there was no mistaking the intensity of emotion.

Satisfaction and something more filled him up.

Lauren loved him.

The question was what to do about it?

## CHAPTER THIRTEEN

LAUREN SAT AT her desk, carefully scrutinizing the event schedule, shifting people around, hiring more where necessary. It was the biggest Hollywood awards ceremony of the season, and By Arrangement would be hosting Obsidian Studio's huge after-party. She expected it to go on way into the next morning.

Usually they wouldn't attempt two events on such a big day, but a valued customer had called two days ago, requesting they handle a brunch for twenty on the day of the awards. Lauren hadn't been able to refuse. So she'd shuffled and shifted, authorized overtime, and wrung miracles out of vendors.

When her phone rang she lifted it to her ear, eyes still on the schedule. "This is Lauren."

"I leave for a week and you run off to New York and get engaged. To *Ray*. I knew there was more to that fling than you were admitting."

"Tori!" Lauren hopped up and closed her door. "I didn't expect to hear from you until you got home."

"I am back—well, in New York anyway. We'll be flying home later today." The second half of her honeymoon she would be attending the awards, and then settling into her new home with Garrett. "And I see I just missed you here. It would have been fun to spend the day together in New York."

"Honeymoon so boring you need company?"

"Uh, that would be *no*." Tori's merry laughter rang over the line. "France was fabulous. We had dinner at the top of the Eifel Tower the night before we left. It was breathtaking."

"So is New York from the crown of the Statue of Liberty. You should check it out if you have time."

"Hmm… So, are you going to tell me about Ray?"

"Oh, Tori. I miss you so much." Lauren forced a calming breath. "But I'm not going to intrude on your honeymoon."

"The only way you're going to do that is if you leave me hanging."

"I'm serious."

"So am I. Garrett went to the gym for a few minutes. Spill, already."

Lauren spilled everything. Taking the pregnancy test at Tori's wedding, Ray's request to go to New York with him, Mamó's announcement of their non-existent engagement, falling in love, Ray freaking at the news of the baby—which, hey, turned out was twins.

Tori let her talk, except for shrieking over news of the twins. In the end she went right to the heart of the matter.

"You've been through a lot in such a short amount of time. I heard you blow by that mention of love. I know you're hurt by his distancing himself, but do you love Ray?"

"Yes. No. I do, but—"

"No buts. Yes or no?"

"It's not that easy," Lauren protested. "I can't, Tori. I thought yes once before, and it was an illusion."

"Love isn't meant to be easy. I almost lost Garrett because I was afraid to trust him. Afraid to trust myself. I let a piece of my past stop me from seeing beyond the surface. I needed to open my eyes and my heart and take that final step into the present."

Lauren remembered. Watching her sister suffer and not

being able to help had been excruciating. But Lauren's situation was different.

"You don't understand. What I feel for Ray is so much more than what I felt for Brad. His reticence *does* hurt. It makes me worry I've given too much of myself away. I can't be in another relationship where I care more than my partner. If it goes wrong with Ray I'm not sure I could find my way back."

"Sis, you're stronger than you think. Brad was able to influence you because you believed you loved him and naturally wanted to please him. You never conceived of someone taking advantage of you in such a way. You're aware now. You need to trust yourself and trust Ray."

Lauren paced in front of her desk. "I don't know if it can work. He's manipulative and he likes his own way."

A snort sounded in her ear, and then Tori demanded, "What man doesn't? Let me ask you this: has he ever coerced you into doing something you didn't want to do?"

The whole New York trip came to mind. But, to be truthful, he'd accepted her refusal. She'd been the one to change her mind. He always seemed to be making plans she had issues with, but when presented with challenges he adapted well.

"Uh-uh." Tori finally cut off Lauren's search for an example. "You told me after we were engaged that you'd seen Garrett and I belonged together."

"I remember. You obviously cared for him, but I didn't want to unduly influence you. If you'd continued to be stubborn I probably would have said something eventually."

"I'm glad to hear you say so. I get the same feeling about you and Ray."

Lauren froze. "You're just saying that to get me to act."

"Maybe, but it's also true. Don't dismiss the significance of the bond just because it's not what you want to hear."

"He's back in town," Lauren volunteered. "Before things blew up between us he asked me to go to the awards show with him."

He'd called and texted every fifteen minutes for the past hour and a half. *Now* he wanted to talk. Finally she'd texted back that she was busy with work and she'd contact him on Monday. His response was that he'd leave a ticket for her at Reception.

"Wow. You've got to go. It would be perfect if we're both there, and then we can go to the party after. It's everything we've been working toward."

"Except for the pre-event work and the estrangement between me and Ray."

"Yeah, well, you need to get over that. You belong together, Lauren."

A deep male rumble sounded in the background. Then Tori's muffled voice.

"Give…minute…talking to Lauren."

A giggle.

"Always…that thought…shower…"

Then she was back.

"Lauren, think about what I said. Trust yourself, girl. The risk is worth the reward."

The happiness in her twin's voice reinforced her claim. She'd given Lauren a lot to think about.

"Hey, don't worry about me. Go take care of your man."

"I do believe I will. See you soon. Oh, and Lauren? If you don't allow yourself to love again, then Brad is still controlling you. And that's just sad."

Unsettled by the call, Lauren returned to her desk and the spreadsheet. Mouse in hand, she stared at the screen.

*"If you don't allow yourself to love again, then Brad is still controlling you."*

Tori's proclamation echoed through Lauren's mind again and again. The concept of him still having any influence on her raked across her senses like fingernails over a blackboard.

Neither did it sit well with her that he might triumph over Ray in any way. It wasn't true. Yet that was what Tori's words implied. Lauren's blood chilled at the very notion of anyone getting that impression, including her. *Especially* her.

She blinked and the schedule spreadsheet came back into view. By sheer strength of will she finished it and handed it off to her assistant, deliberately leaving Tori and herself off the assignment delegation. They'd both be there, but this way Tori got to enjoy herself. And Lauren could be wherever she was needed.

After the success of Obsidian Studio's event at the Hollywood Hills Film Festival, Obsidian's after-party was being hyped as the event not to miss. It was the pinnacle of By Arrangement's achievements. Not even her current heartache could steal her pride in their accomplishments. This party signified everything she'd been working for.

Logistics-wise, there really was no reason she couldn't attend the awards with Ray. With the adjustments she'd made, her assistant and Tori's should be able to handle both events without the company's owners. Plus, the two of them would be attending the Obsidian Studio party and could step in if needed.

But it was to be *her* night, *her* success, and she needed to be in the midst of it…

Still, she remembered the thrill when he'd asked her to attend the awards with him—the longing to go. Not because it put her closer to her career goals, but because she wanted to support him. His brilliance deserved to be honored and something instinctual in her demanded she be by his side.

Except the day had to belong to *her*. If she gave it up, did that prove she was right back to putting a man's desires before her own?

Not forgetting the fact that the world believed her to be his fiancée. How could she walk the red carpet at his side, pretending all the time they were together, when in truth they'd never been further apart?

By Sunday morning Lauren still hadn't made up her mind. Her emotions rode a teeter-totter ride—up one moment, down the next. She went from wanting to support Ray to needing the validation of self-worth that would come with working the party. Giving it up would diminish her power. Which was exactly what she feared happening.

Of course Ray completely ignored her attempt to put him off until Monday. At ten a courier arrived in her office with an envelope. Inside was her ticket to the award ceremony and a note:

*It'll be a crush at the theater. I wanted to save you the trouble of going after the ticket. I'm hoping you'll be my lucky charm.*
*Ray*

His lucky charm. No pressure there. And he didn't fool her—he wanted to make it easy so she had no excuse for not doing what he wanted.

Yeah, *that* was going to work. But along with annoyance came a little thrill of flattery. He really had no need for her to join him. He usually walked the red carpet alone. With her along the attention would flip from the potential of his movie winning to their faux engagement. She would literally be stealing his limelight.

An hour later another courier arrived, carrying three large stacked boxes tied with five-inch-wide red ribbon and a huge red bow.

"No. N. O. I'm not accepting this," she told the wiry teenager in a gray tee and jeans. "Take it back."

"Sorry, ma'am."

*Ma'am*? Seriously? Okay, yeah, she'd be a mother soon, but she was way too young to be called "ma'am."

"There's a no return flag. I'm not allowed to take it back." He gave her a big grin. "Got a *nice* tip, though. You enjoy, now."

He practically ran out the door. No doubt in a hurry to spend his *"nice* tip".

Hands on hips, body and soul at odds, she sighed, eying the stacked boxes. Her fingers itched to tear into the ribbon to see what the white boxes hid. A dress, for certain, and possibly shoes. A weakness of hers. But if she saw, she'd want. And he was manipulating her. Seducing her with niceties and beautiful things into going with him instead of working.

And he was getting to her. But she lacked the skill-set to spend hours in his company pretending there weren't unresolved issues between them. If nothing else the New York trip had proved that beyond all doubt.

She tore into the boxes. *Temptation, thy name is Ray.* And, yes, the biggest held a dress. An Eve Gardner. Oh, he was good.

She'd tried this black gown on in New York and it had fit like a dream, with a fitted bodice with narrow straps and a square neckline low enough to display the rising swell of her breasts. The dress had clung to her curves, the material flowing over her body with a soft sheen. Too daring for the mayor's reception...tame by Hollywood standards.

The smallest box held shoes—strappy silver heels, with rhinestones and a lifted sole that made her drool.

No fair. He knew her too well. And he'd hit her weaknesses dead target.

The last box surprised her. It held the red leather jacket he'd bought her in New York. The one it had broken her heart to leave behind. She clutched it to her like she'd found an old friend.

A note slipped to the table.

*Something to wear. And shoes, because a special
dress deserves new shoes. Or so Kyla assured me.
No lingerie, because frankly I don't care if you wear
any. And the jacket because I plan to buy you many
things through the years. Best to get used to it now.
Ray*

She folded the jacket and put it back in the box. Tucked
the dress and shoes out of sight too. His reference to
"through the years" yanked at her heart strings. A master
at setting scenes, his message today hinted at a future together. But she didn't dare assume.

She fingered the phone in her skirt pocket, longing to
call him.

But, no. Their conversation, when they had it, needed
to be in person. If she called he'd try to charm her into
going to the awards and all her progress would be lost.
Best to tough it out.

A task made more difficult when the staff spied the
boxes and demanded to see their contents. Oohs and aahs
echoed through the room, but what really cut through her
resolve was when her assistant, Maria, pulled her aside
and assured Lauren she could handle the party.

"I've learned so much from you. I can do this. You
should go to the awards—have fun."

"This is a big event. It's not fair to ask you—"

"You're not asking. You've trained us to be a well-
oiled machine. You should take advantage of what you've
wrought and live the life the rest of us only dream about."

"Thanks, Maria. I'll think about it." An easy promise
to make as her thoughts revolved around little else.

Just before noon Lauren stood at her desk, gathering her
things to move over to the Lowes Hotel—the venue for
tonight's party. It was adjacent to the theater which was
the home of the awards ceremony.

She glanced up at the sound of the bell to see two men in their display showroom. One wore an expensive suit and the other a security guard's uniform.

Smoothing her hands over her blue skirt, she went to greet them. When they saw her they advanced to meet her. On closer view, she noted that the guard was armed and the man in the suit carried a metal case handcuffed to his wrist.

*Good gracious, Ray, what have you done?*

"Gentlemen, I'm Lauren Randall—how can I help you?"

"Yes, Ms. Randall. I have a delivery for you. Might we go somewhere more private?" asked the suited man.

"This will have to do." Her office wouldn't hold the three of them.

"Very well." He set the briefcase on the nearest display table. "May I see some identification, please?"

"And if I say no…?"

"I've been instructed to stay with you until I've made the delivery."

"Of course you have." She went to her desk, grabbed her purse, returned to show him her ID.

Suit Man opened the case and lifted out a long, flat velvet jewelry box. With practiced ceremony he opened the hinged case and displayed the dazzling contents.

"The Sabina of the Claudia Collection, House of Brandia."

Diamond layers about an inch wide formed a pattern that reminded her of leaves. The avant-garde neck-piece was designed to flow around the neck and almost meet at the front. One point, formed of three oval rubies, would hit the center of her chest above her breasts, then the collar would wrap around her neck and the second ruby-tipped end would stop two inches above the first point, leaving an inch of skin between the two points. Matching earrings completed the set.

Speechless, Lauren simply stared. The set had a name— the Sabina. She loved the avant-garde design of the pieces.

But she couldn't wear them. Not in a million years. Not if its delivery required an armed guard escort. This went so far beyond the red jacket it was ridiculous.

What was Ray *thinking*?

"And there's this." Suit held out a small box.

Lauren's heart jumped into her throat. A tremble revealed her state as she reached for the ring box. It shook in the palm of her hand.

Suit reached into his front breast pocket. "Mr. Donovan also sent a missive." He offered the envelope with a flourish.

*Missive*? The dude clearly liked his drama.

As did Ray.

"You need to take this back," she informed Suit, and included Security Guard just to cover all bases. "I can't be responsible for this."

"May I suggest you read the letter, Ms. Randall?"

The hefty guard nodded.

Of course they'd stick together.

Turning away from the two men, she tore into the envelope.

*Dynamite*

   *Don't freak out. The jewels are on loan. Just a few baubles to add to your enjoyment of the night. I hope you like them. When I saw the necklace I thought of you. A special piece for a special woman.*

   *The ring is my grandmother's wedding ring. She gave it to me fifteen years ago to give to the woman I would marry. Camilla didn't deserve it. I couldn't give it to her.*

   *Will you wear it tonight? With you by my side I'll be a winner regardless of the results revealed on stage. Afterward we'll go to your party and I can watch you work. So sexy.*

   *I love you, Lauren. I want to live my life with you*

*and our twins and our future children. I admit it
took me a while to get to this point. But it feels right.*

*We have much to talk about. Much to look for-
ward to.*

*Tonight our journey begins.*
*With all my love,*
*Ray.*

Lauren opened the ring box, drew in a sharp breath.
Stunning—just stunning. An oval of small diamonds
framed three raised round diamonds, the middle one bigger than the top and bottom gems. Two rows of diamonds
flowed off each side into a platinum band.

It fit perfectly on her finger.

She was so lost.

From the vantage point of the Panorama Suite of the Lowes
Hotel Lauren watched the frantic activity down below as
the Hollywood elite started to arrive for the big night. The
limo line would be non-stop for the next four hours as the
five-hundred-foot red carpet and then the theater filled.
The people filling the seven hundred bleacher seats had
been in place for hours.

Behind her the thirty-five-hundred square foot suite,
complete with baby grand piano, was ready except for the
food and servers—but this was just the escape route, or
more accurately the end-game.

Downstairs her team was putting the final touches on
the transformation of the main ballroom into an upscale
club with a sexy edge. Music, dancing, and live perfor-
mances would take the party into the wee hours.

Along with the Panorama Suite, Obsidian had taken a
full floor of rooms. Some were for performers, others for
executives, and half were set aside as changing rooms.
Many stars liked to change after the awards. Lauren had
convinced Obsidian to offer them a place to do so.

Her own finery was spread out on the bed in her room.

The problem? She still ping-ponged about whether to go with Ray or stay and work.

She'd texted him not to send a car for her; said she was working at the Lowes. Vague, much?

He'd proposed, sent her a beautiful ring she had yet to remove, had been the first to admit his feelings. Pretty brave, considering she hadn't spoken to him since leaving New York. She owed him a real response.

More importantly, she owed herself an honest response.

"Hey." Tori's heels clicked on the hardwood floor. "We're heading out. Garrett wants to get a quick bite to eat before we meet up with Ray in an hour."

"Have fun," Lauren urged without turning around.

"I'm still hoping you'll join us." Warm arms enfolded her in a hug. "I wish it were as clear to you as it is to me. You love him, he loves you, you're having twins. You belong together."

Lauren curled her arms over Tori's, savoring the familiar touch, the unconditional love.

"I wish it were that simple, too."

Suddenly bigger arms, stronger arms, enveloped the both of them as Garrett added his support. His deep voice sounded close to her ear.

"He's the best man I know."

"Of course you think so." Tears welled up. A half-sob escaped as her breath hitched. "He's your best friend."

"Yeah, but you're my sister now," Garrett said. "I wouldn't tell you something I don't believe to be true."

"Thank you."

His support touched her. A loving family was a new concept for him, so she knew what reaching out cost him. She turned around and hugged them both.

"I love you." She pulled free. "Now, go. I'll see you later."

After a last hug from Tori, they left.

At the door, Tori looked back. "Get out of your head. As long as you're replaying the same loop you're going to get the same answer." She waved and was gone.

Get out of her head? If only she could. Unbidden, Tori's words from yesterday came back to Lauren.

*"If you don't allow yourself to love again, then Brad is still controlling you."*

She clenched her hands until her nails bit into her palms. No way was she letting that happen. So enough, already. No more internal fighting. She needed to let go of what she *should* do and focus on what she *wanted* to do. In other words: get out of her head.

Eyes closed, taking deep breaths, she let it all go. Counting…ten in, ten out. Three times. It was the most peace she'd had in hours. Days.

Her hand found her stomach and she focused on the twins growing within her. She imagined holding them in her arms, guiding them through their first steps, trying to decipher twin-talk, taking them to preschool, ballet classes, T-ball, puppy dogs, high school drama and graduation.

She stopped there because she had her answer.

Through all her visions of laughter and chatter, pirouettes and proms, doggies and dugouts Ray stood by her side, guiding, dancing, scooping, and beaming: a family.

By her side. Not leading or directing, but sharing—a partner in life.

Tension drained out of her as she accepted the truth.

She'd been doing to him what she'd feared he'd do to her: punishing him for another's sins. She'd worried she'd lose herself to Ray's dominant personality as she had to Brad's. *Not going to happen.* As Tori had said, Lauren was aware. She knew what to watch for. The problem was she hadn't been paying attention.

Ray was a self-confident, take-charge kind of man, used to getting his way and directing events to his liking. Yes, he manipulated—but he did it in your face. No snarky, sneaky moves for him. And he'd never guilted or maneuvered her into doing something she didn't want to do.

That had been Brad's style. Always using faux understanding or disappointment as a tool to make her do as he wanted. He'd made it seem as if she were deciding to do something when he'd actually used her emotions against her to get his way. Her desire to compromise had eventually become habit, until she'd always deferred to his will.

In truth, the two men couldn't be more different.

She loved Ray. There was nothing wrong with wanting to be with him on this exciting day in his career. In fact it was normal.

With her decision made, she felt the anxiety surrounding her work disappear. Yes, this event represented everything she and Tori had been working toward. But just because she wasn't overseeing every little detail it didn't take any of the responsibility or success away from her. She'd built the business into what it was. And she'd be there. Available to assist if needed. The best of both worlds.

Ray knew how important her career was to her. He'd never try to get in the way of it. In fact he'd written something in that last note. What was it? She'd read right over it, too stunned by everything else in the message.

She found her purse and the note tucked inside. Now she was free of conflict the romance of it struck her anew. He'd honored her request not to contact her until Monday while completely disregarding it at the same time.

Here it was:

*Afterward, we'll go to your party and I can watch you work. So sexy.*

Her heart swelled even fuller. He was the best man *she* knew, too.

A glance at the clock revealed an hour had passed since

Tori and Garrett had left. They'd be starting on the red carpet soon.

She reached for the zipper on her dress, yanked it down as she kicked out of her heels. *Hurry!* Thank the angels her hair and make-up were already done.

The beep of her phone announced a text. From Ray.

Lauren. I'm at the theater and you're not with me. I understand. We have a lot to talk about. This changes nothing for me. I hold you in my heart, so you are with me even when you're not. It just means we'll have one more thing to celebrate tomorrow when we do get together. I'll see you at the party. You couldn't keep me away. Fair warning, Dynamite: Monday starts at midnight. I love you. Ray

Incorrigible.

Grinning, she wiggled and her dress hit the floor. Seconds later her underthings joined the dress. Naked, she slipped into the sexy gown. So naughty—but, oh, yeah, Ray deserved a thrill for the silent treatment she'd subjected him to all day long.

Ten minutes later she rode the elevator down and walked over to the theater. The crush of people grew thicker as she neared the red carpet. The public pressed against the barricades while the press jockeyed for position and Security tried to maintain control.

She finally reached the entrance and found more chaos. Someone took her ticket and sent her to the aisle that led directly into the theater. She was tempted to meet him inside, but he wanted her by his side. And she wanted to be there, too.

Just then she spied a friendly security officer she knew from events they'd both worked. Waving, she caught the plump African American woman's attention.

"Ms. Randall—wow, you are *rockin'* that dress. You need to be on this side of the carpet."

"Thanks. That's why I called you over. My date has already started down the carpet. Can you take me to him?"

"So it's true? You're engaged to Ray Donovan?"

"Yes!" Lauren held out her hand, flashing her ring. "I really need to get to him."

"You sure do, girlfriend." The woman ran a hand over her red dreads. "How can I help?"

"Can you take me to him?"

"Hmm. I really can't leave my post."

"Oh." Disappoint bit deep. "Okay. I guess I'll wait for him inside."

"Can't have that. You need to get to your man. Hang on."

The officer stepped away and spoke into her radio.

Seconds and then minutes ticked by. Lauren chafed under the wait. Finally a man the size of a linebacker came along, clearly someone with authority, and talked to her friend. He glanced at Lauren, then approached her.

He looked at the necklace she wore, consulted his clipboard. "Is that the Sabina?"

"Yes." Her hand flew to the jewels at her neck. "From the Claudia Collection, House of Brandia."

He nodded. "Ms. Randall, we're going to get you through." He unhooked the rope barrier and let her pass. "Bonnie will lead you to Mr. Donovan. He's about a quarter ways up the carpet."

"Thank you." Lauren followed Bonnie as she started up the carpet.

The red carpet worked efficiently by having the press and cameras on one side and the stars on the other as they strolled from photo point to photo point. To keep from photo-bombing half of Hollywood, Bonnie led Lauren down the press side, which involved evading cables, cameras, and lampstands as well as many members of the press.

Threading their way through, they caused a bit of disruption. A buzz started behind her and moved forward with them as she was recognized.

"We're causing a spectacle," Lauren told Bonnie. "Maybe I should just meet him inside."

"This is Hollywood, girlfriend. Everyone loves a good spectacle."

"Then let's hurry."

Picking up her skirts, she took off as fast as her heels allowed.

Ray stepped up to the next microphone in a long line of microphones. He greeted the host by name and complimented her on her dress. Gave silent thanks she didn't ask who he was wearing.

No, she went right for the kill.

"Ray Donovan, you have a chance to sweep the season with *War Zone* tonight. And we got news of your engagement this week. Where *is* the lucky woman? With the stakes so high for you, we were hoping to see her on your arm."

"Of course she wants to be here. But, as owner of the hottest event company in Hollywood, today is a busy day for her."

"I imagine." The woman turned to the camera. "We're talking about Lauren Randall of By Arrangements, which has been applauded for great premier productions. Her sister just married Obsidian Studios owner Garrett Black. These lucky twins are snapping up Hollywood royalty."

"I don't know about royalty," Ray demurred. Mention of the newlyweds had him looking around, hoping for a save. They were stuck one mic back. "Garrett is a good friend." He kept it simple. "Now we'll be family."

Or so he planned.

He hoped he hadn't put Lauren off with his persistence today. No lie: he had freaked when she'd refused to talk to him. Not that he didn't deserve it. Now he knew what *she'd* gone through while he'd kept her waiting in New York.

He'd hoped the ring would sway her, because he really wanted her by his side—now and forever.

"Well, good luck tonight." The woman waved, then put a hand to her ear. "What's that?"

Ray got the sign to move on, which suited him fine. He turned away, rolled his eyes when he caught Garrett's stare.

"Wait. Ray!" The woman caught Ray's arm. Then quickly dropped it as she flushed red. "There's a disturbance on the red carpet. It seems Lauren is trying to catch up with you. Why don't you wait…?"

Joy swelled up, lending Ray height as he leapt off the dais and backtracked to reach Lauren.

Progress moved at a snail's pace. He traveled against the flow of humanity, causing a commotion, and making it worse were all the friends and colleagues who wanted to greet and congratulate him.

All he wanted was to get to Lauren.

He picked up his pace.

And then he saw her. He came to a dead stop, awed by her beauty, by her grace, by her radiance. The dress hugged her curves, displaying her delectable cleavage, while the jewels drew attention to her uniqueness.

His soul shouted, *Mine!*

She looked up, saw him, and her face lit up.

Lauren looked up and there was Ray. Finally. Her heart sang. Feet moving with grace and balance, she danced her way to him and launched herself into his arms.

Applause broke out around them. She barely heard it, too busy kissing her man.

"You made it," he said against her lips.

"I wouldn't miss it for the world."

Neither spoke of the awards show. "I love you," he breathed into her ear, arms locked around her in an embrace meant to last forever. "I was punishing you for so many reasons. All wrong."

"Me too." She couldn't let him go—never wanted to let go ever again. "I was afraid to give you too much power because I gave too much to Brad. But you've never taken from me. You've always empowered me to be more, better, sexier. I love you, Ray Donovan, with all my heart and with all my head."

Lights and clicks flashed and binged from every direction.

He pulled back to frame her face in hands strong and sure, his love on full display. "Will you marry me? I'll get you your own ring—"

"Shh." She pressed a finger to his mouth, held up her hand so Mamó's ring flashed in the afternoon light. "This ring is perfect. It comes with a history of love."

His jaw clenched and then he was kissing her again, long and soft, with tenderness and devotion. She sighed inside, seeing the caress as a testament to his hope for the future.

He lifted his head, stared into her eyes, his eyes promising everything his kiss had just declared. "I wish we were alone."

"Not me. The world is watching, and I want everyone to know you're mine. Time to say goodbye to your bachelorhood, Mr. Donovan."

His eyes lit up at the challenge. "My pleasure, Mrs. Donovan-to-be."

He took her hand, kissed Mamó's ring, and turned them both toward the waiting crowd of spectators and press.

"Congratulate me, everyone. Lauren Randall has agreed to be my bride."

# EPILOGUE

LAUREN REACHED THE DOOR, checked in both directions down the hallway and slipped inside. She flipped on the light and grinned at the spread she found already set up on the counter next to the washing machine.

Holding her extended belly, she waddled over to inspect the goodies. Cheese and fruit, some roast beef from last night's dinner. And—oh, yeah—pickles. She stole one and popped it in her mouth. Such a cliché craving for a pregnant woman—but, hey, clichés got to be known for a reason.

She started when the door opened behind her. Just Ray, sneaking in. He carried a bottle of sparkling apple juice and two glasses.

He came to her, bent over the twins, and kissed her softly. "Hello."

"Hello. Did anyone see you?"

"Nope. Tori and Garrett just got here. That'll give Mamó and your mother someone else to focus on for at least half an hour."

The newlyweds had announced that they were expecting at the last family get-together in July. Lauren's mom was in heaven, with both her girls married and starting families. She and Mamó had become best friends. Everyone was gathered at her and Ray's place now because she was scheduled to have the twins in two days.

"This was a great idea." She settled into the chair he

pulled out and opened for her, shifted trying to get comfortable. Her back had been bothering her all day. "I love the support and having everyone about. But I have to say I miss having you all to myself."

With so many people in the house, alone time had become impossible. So when Ray had suggested a laundry room tryst she'd jumped at it. The small room had become their little hideout whenever the house was full. Nobody looked for them there.

He sat next to her and she leaned against his strength. She rubbed her belly. "Two girls. Are you ready?"

"No." A touch of panic sounded in the one word. "Maybe we can put it off for another week. Maybe a month."

She laughed, then winced as a twinge rolled up her back. She groaned. "You wouldn't do that to me, would you?"

"I guess not." He watched her carefully. "Are you okay?"

"Just tired. You may not be ready, but I am. And so are the girls."

"They were restless last night."

"Tell me about it. I wasn't able to get comfortable all night. Two more days. I can hardly wait." She sympathized with his nervousness, but she'd moved on to the *I want them out of me* stage.

"Are you hungry?" He served her food and juice, watched over her every move. His care showed his devotion to her and their girls.

"You take such good care of me."

"Not too controlling for you?"

"Marrying you was the best decision I ever made," she answered, without looking up from the tray he held for her perusal.

It scared her sometimes, how close she'd come to walking away from him. Thank goodness for his persistence.

She picked up a thin piece of provolone, but almost lost her hold when the tray was yanked away. "Hey!"

"Hey, back." He took the cheese, tossed it toward the tray, kissed her long and deep. "I love you. Marrying you was the best thing I ever did."

She was so lucky, so loved. "Oh."

"Oh, you love me too?"

"No. I mean yes. I love you. But *oh* because my water just broke."

She watched him carefully, waiting for the hint of panic from earlier to take hold. It never came.

Ray went into director mode, herding her downstairs, putting the family to work gathering her suitcase, getting the car, the baby gear. Never once did he let her go. She relaxed and let him do his thing, confident he had everything under control.

Four hours later she cradled her first daughter in her arms. Looking down into her tiny features, she felt such love flowing through her she didn't think it could get any bigger, be any stronger. Then she looked up and saw Ray next to her, cooing at a second little girl bundled in pink, and her emotions doubled in an instant.

The doors opened and family flowed into the room to admire the new additions.

Amid the chaos Ray lifted blue eyes to hers and mouthed, *I love you.*

And her love grew even bigger.

\* \* \* \* \*

# MILLS & BOON®
## Hardback – February 2015

## ROMANCE

| | |
|---|---|
| The Redemption of Darius Sterne | Carole Mortimer |
| The Sultan's Harem Bride | Annie West |
| Playing by the Greek's Rules | Sarah Morgan |
| Innocent in His Diamonds | Maya Blake |
| To Wear His Ring Again | Chantelle Shaw |
| The Man to Be Reckoned With | Tara Pammi |
| Claimed by the Sheikh | Rachael Thomas |
| Delucca's Marriage Contract | Abby Green |
| Her Brooding Italian Boss | Susan Meier |
| The Heiress's Secret Baby | Jessica Gilmore |
| A Pregnancy, a Party & a Proposal | Teresa Carpenter |
| Best Friend to Wife and Mother? | Caroline Anderson |
| The Sheikh Doctor's Bride | Meredith Webber |
| A Baby to Heal Their Hearts | Kate Hardy |
| One Hot Desert Night | Kristi Gold |
| Snowed In with Her Ex | Andrea Laurence |
| Cowgirls Don't Cry | Silver James |
| Terms of a Texas Marriage | Lauren Canan |

## MEDICAL

| | |
|---|---|
| A Date with Her Valentine Doc | Melanie Milburne |
| It Happened in Paris... | Robin Gianna |
| Temptation in Paradise | Joanna Neil |
| The Surgeon's Baby Secret | Amber McKenzie |

# MILLS & BOON®
## Large Print – February 2015

## ROMANCE

| | |
|---|---|
| **An Heiress for His Empire** | Lucy Monroe |
| **His for a Price** | Caitlin Crews |
| **Commanded by the Sheikh** | Kate Hewitt |
| **The Valquez Bride** | Melanie Milburne |
| **The Uncompromising Italian** | Cathy Williams |
| **Prince Hafiz's Only Vice** | Susanna Carr |
| **A Deal Before the Altar** | Rachael Thomas |
| **The Billionaire in Disguise** | Soraya Lane |
| **The Unexpected Honeymoon** | Barbara Wallace |
| **A Princess by Christmas** | Jennifer Faye |
| **His Reluctant Cinderella** | Jessica Gilmore |

## HISTORICAL

| | |
|---|---|
| **Zachary Black: Duke of Debauchery** | Carole Mortimer |
| **The Truth About Lady Felkirk** | Christine Merrill |
| **The Courtesan's Book of Secrets** | Georgie Lee |
| **Betrayed by His Kiss** | Amanda McCabe |
| **Falling for Her Captor** | Elisabeth Hobbes |

## MEDICAL

| | |
|---|---|
| **Tempted by Her Boss** | Scarlet Wilson |
| **His Girl From Nowhere** | Tina Beckett |
| **Falling For Dr Dimitriou** | Anne Fraser |
| **Return of Dr Irresistible** | Amalie Berlin |
| **Daring to Date Her Boss** | Joanna Neil |
| **A Doctor to Heal Her Heart** | Annie Claydon |